He laughed  a little bit of a jealous streak," he teased.

"I do not!"

"Yes
fing
curr
it,"
I'm
really
getti

The _____ her face. His touch was heated, fire coursed through her palm, up the length of her arm and exploded with a vengeance through her body. A tingle ran down her spine and back up, the sensations a shiver away from orgasmic.

She suddenly pulled her hand from his, color heating her cheeks. Turning her body around, she lay back against him, resting her head in his lap. She pulled a grape from the bunch in her hands and slid it into her mouth.

Dear Reader,

The Stallion-Boudreaux clan continue to thrill me! I love these two families, and telling their stories has been so fulfilling.

Tuscan Heat brings us back to the Boudreaux side of the family alliance. Donovan Boudreaux takes us to one of my favorite places in the whole wide world! Everything about Italy screams romance and love, and Donovan finds it in the most unlikely manner.

As I've said many times before, there could be no Boudreaux story without that foundation of family, friends and faith. Like his siblings, Donovan is very much his own man. He's a tad conservative and maybe even a little introverted. Gianna Martelli and her big, bold personality are a formidable challenge. She's fire to his ice, and together they will melt your heart! I so hope you enjoy their journey as they find love.

Thank you so much for your continued support. I am humbled by all the love you keep showing me, my characters and our stories. I know that none of this would be possible without you.

Until the next time, please take care and may God's blessings be with you always.

With much love,

Deborah Fletcher Mello

deborahmello.blogspot.com

Tuscan Heat

DEBORAH
FLETCHER
MELLO

HARLEQUIN® KIMANI™ ROMANCE

To my Muse
for keeping me dreaming.
You make my heart sing!

Recycling programs
for this product may
not exist in your area.

ISBN-13: 978-0-373-86433-1

Tuscan Heat

H HARLEQUIN®
™ www.Harlequin.com

Printed in U.S.A.

Deborah Fletcher Mello has been writing since forever and can't imagine herself doing anything else. Her first romance novel, *Take Me to Heart*, earned her a 2004 Romance Slam Jam nomination for Best New Author. In 2005 she received Book of the Year and Favorite Heroine nominations for her novel *The Right Side of Love*, and in 2009 she won an RT Reviewer's Choice Award for her ninth novel, *Tame a Wild Stallion*. With each new book Deborah continues to create unique storylines and memorable characters.

Born and raised in Connecticut, Deborah now considers home to be wherever the moment moves her.

Books by Deborah Fletcher Mello

Harlequin Kimani Romance

Visit the Author Profile page at
Harlequin.com for more titles.

THE BOUDREAUX FAMILY TREE

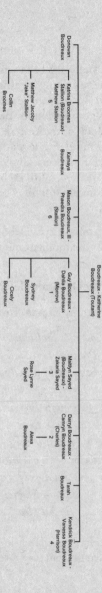

Mason "Senior" Boudreaux - Katherine Boudreaux (Toutant)

Donovan Boudreaux

Katrina Broomes Stallion (Boudreaux) - Matthew Stallion
5
- Matthew Jacoby "Jake" Stallion
- Collin Broomes

Kamaya Boudreaux

Mason Boudreaux, III - Phaedra Boudreaux (Stallion)
6

Guy Boudreaux - Dahlia Boudreaux (Morrow)
1
- Sydney Boudreaux
- Cicely Boudreaux

Maitlyn Sayed (Boudreaux) - Zakaria Sayed
3
- Rose Lynne Sayed

Darryl Boudreaux - Camryn Boudreaux (Charles)
2
- Alexa Boudreaux

Tarah Boudreaux

Kendrick Boudreaux - Vanessa Boudreaux (Harrison)
4

BOUDREAUX FAMILY SERIES
1. Passionate Premiere
2. Truly Yours
3. Hearts Afire
4. Twelve Days of Pleasure
5. Seduced By A Stallion (The Stallion Series)
6. Forever A Stallion (The Stallion Series)

Chapter 1

She and her sister were identical twins, and most people were never able to tell the two women apart. But Gianna Martelli had taken a pair of scissors to her sibling Carina's dark locks, cutting the young woman's waist-length tresses to pixie short. Carina's natural curls were suddenly less abundant as she stood in the center of the room, her head waving slowly from side to side to show off her new hairdo to their family.

"Wow!" Graham Porter exclaimed, his dark eyes shifting back and forth between the two women. "Wow!"

"What's that mean?" Carina questioned, her eyebrows lifted as she tossed her husband a look. "Why do you keep saying wow like that?" A wave of panic flashed across her face. "You don't like it!"

He met the look his wife was giving him, holding

his hands up defensively. "No... I mean yes... I do! It's just unexpected," he said, turning to his father-in-law for assistance. "What do you think, Franco?"

Franco Martelli grinned. "It's lovely, daughter. But it's a definite change. And like Graham said, it's unexpected! I think what your husband is trying to say is that you've surprised us, is all."

"I told you to trust me," Gianna said as Carina smiled, pulling her hands through the new short length of her hair. "It really does look great!"

"Are you going to cut yours, too?" Franco asked, turning in his seat to stare at Gianna.

The young woman shrugged. "I was thinking about it, but Carina doesn't want me to."

"I want us to look different," Carina said. "Just for a little while. No one will mix us up now."

Gianna rolled her eyes skyward, tossing the extensive length of her own dark waves over her shoulder. "It's been forever since anyone last got us confused."

"Last week at the market, Mrs. Falco thought I was you."

"Mrs. Falco is half-blind," Gianna said with an eye roll. "She gets *papà* and Graham mixed up!"

Graham chuckled as he rose to his feet, moving to his wife's side. He leaned down to kiss her cheek. "It's a very flattering style on you, sweetheart. I really like it," he said softly. "You look beautiful!" He trailed a finger across Carina's cheek, and she smiled brightly as he leaned in to kiss her lips.

Gianna threw the two a look, the faintest hint of jealousy furrowing her brow. She blew a low sigh. "You two need to get a room," she quipped. She rose from her seat and moved toward the door. "I'll be in my office. Some of us have work to do."

"Speaking of," Carina said, "I sorted your mail and typed up your notes. And your agent called. She needs to speak with you about the changes in your next contract."

"I don't have a next contract. I told you to tell her I'm not interested in what they're offering."

"I did, which is why she wants to speak with you."

Gianna nodded. "I'll call her," she said, trying to ignore the gentle caresses passing between her sister and brother-in-law. The couple's very public displays of affection were often distracting and unsettling, the love the two shared enviable. Gianna couldn't help but wish that she had what they had. With one last wave of her hand she turned and disappeared from the room.

Behind the closed door of her office, Gianna ran her fingers through her own thick tresses, pulling the wealth of her hair up into a high bun. She found herself wishing that she'd cut her own hair first, motivated by the effort it took to maintain the lengthy locks. That, and she found herself in want of a change. One that might bring a man into her life with a slow hand that glided like silk across her bare skin. She blew a low sigh as she turned to stare out the window to the landscape outside.

The sun was shining brightly, and she had full view of the family's vineyards. Their family home was situated in the Ombrone Valley, one of the most beautiful stretches of countryside in Italy. She stared out to the Chianti vines, the cornfields and the lengthy rows of cypress trees. In the distance the expanse of chestnut forests reached up to kiss the bright blue sky. The view paid homage to unparalleled art, the land a masterpiece of blessings. For a brief moment Gianna sat staring at the beauty, lost in her thoughts as the morning's bright rays peeked through the window to kiss the round of her high cheekbones.

She blew one last sigh as she spun around in her leather executive's chair toward her computer. Powering up the device, she waited for the unit to engage then typed in her password. Minutes later she stared at a blank screen, unable to decide in what direction she planned to take her next story. Writer's block had suddenly crept in with a vengeance. When nothing came, she swung her chair around to stare back outside.

Donovan Boudreaux found the pomp and circumstance of the Catholic ceremony somewhat sobering. He was standing at the altar of Saint Patrick's Church in New Orleans holding his niece, Cecily Boudreaux, in his arms. The infant was being christened, she and her twin brother, Sydney, both receiving the sacrament of spiritual cleansing and rebirth. Light shimmered through the stained glass that enclosed the building's front turret.

He fought the urge to yawn as Father Charles Dussouy made the sign of the cross in front of one baby and then the other. He stared down into the infant's sweet face as the priest announced her Christian name, sprinkled holy water over the child's head and welcomed her into the congregation. She never once opened her eyes, barely shifting her small body when the water saturated her curls. Her brother, on the other hand, screamed at the top of his small lungs.

Donovan grinned as he and his brother Kendrick exchanged a look. Kendrick was rocking young Sydney vigorously, trying his very best to calm the baby down. But Sydney wasn't having any of it, no ounce of consolation from his uncle and godfather bringing him any comfort. It wasn't until the matriarch of the family, Katherine Boudreaux, lifted her grandchild from her son's arms did the little guy finally settle down as she snuggled him against her chest. There was something about their mother's touch that put them all at ease, and as each of her children watched, it made them all smile.

The private ceremony was over almost as quickly as it had begun. After the priest wished them well and disappeared from the sanctuary, the family stood in a protective circle around the twins, who'd been returned to their parents' arms.

Mason "Senior" Boudreaux, the family patriarch, cleared his throat, swiping at a tear that lingered in the corners of his dark eyes. "Your mama and I are glad that all you kids could make it home to celebrate these babies," he said, his tone low. The man's gaze swept around the circle.

The eldest Boudreaux child patted his namesake's broad shoulder. "Where else would we be, Senior? You know once you and Mama give the command we follow orders!" Mason Boudreaux III said.

His siblings laughed, their heads nodding in agreement. Donovan leaned to kiss his mother's cheek, his arms wrapped around her shoulders as he hugged her close. His own eyes roved from one face to the other. There was no escaping the Boudreaux lineage. Their distinctive features hinted of an African-Asian ancestry, with their slight angular eyes, thin noses, high cheek lines and full, pouty lips. Side by side they were a kaleidoscope of colorations that ranged from burnt umber to milk chocolate.

His brother Mason, who could have passed for his twin, stood at his side. The low lines of their closely cropped haircuts complemented their distinctive facial features. Mason's wife, Phaedra, clutched his elbow on his other side. Then there was his very pregnant sister, Maitlyn, and her husband, Zakaria Sayed. Maitlyn was the second child and oldest girl in the Boudreaux family. Standing beside them was his sister Katrina, who was a year younger than Donovan, with her husband, Matthew Stallion, and their two sons, Collin and Jacoby, or Baby Jake, as he was affectionately called. On his right side stood his younger brother Darryl, and Darryl's wife, Camryn, who held their newborn baby, Alexa Michelle, in her arms. The twins, Kendrick and Kamaya were next, Kamaya linked arm in arm with her baby sister, Tarah, and Kendrick's wife, Vanessa. His brother Guy, and Guy's wife, Dahlia, the twins' parents, closed their family circle. In that moment, the love between them all billowed like the sweetest breeze all around.

"Can we please go eat now?" Tarah suddenly whined. "This lovefest has made me hungry."

Katherine shook her head. "I declare, child! You are always hungry."

"I would really like to know how you stay so thin!" Kamaya exclaimed, her head waving.

"Good genes," Tarah said with a soft giggle.

Maitlyn rolled her eyes, slapping a hand against her hips. "We have those same genes, so I don't think that's it," she said with a warm chuckle.

They all headed in the direction of the exit and home. Minutes later the joy and laughter continued at the Boudreaux family's Broadway Street house. The food was abundant, plates overflowing as the family all caught up, conversation sweeping from one room to the other.

"I like the name Rose. Rose Lynne Sayed," Maitlyn was saying, her hand gliding in a tight circle across her abdomen. "Although Zak is still insisting we're having a boy!" she said, leaning in to whisper with her sisters. "He even told the technician that did the ultrasound that she didn't know what she was talking about."

Kamaya laughed. "At least it's not twins!"

"I wouldn't mind having twins," Tarah said. "A boy and a girl. You get it all done in one shot. Dahlia never has to be pregnant again. How perfect is that? You, on the other hand, might have to do it again to get a boy. Maybe even twice."

"If I had thought that way after Kendrick and Kamaya were born, you wouldn't be here," their mother interjected as she joined in the conversation. She took the seat beside Tarah, giving her daughter's ponytail a playful tug.

Kamaya laughed. "I know!"

Katherine turned her attention to Donovan, who was leaning against the home's brick fireplace, a glass of red wine in his hand. "So, Donovan, what's going on with you? What's the big news you wanted to share?"

"Yeah, Don Juan! Are you engaged? Pregnant? What?" Tarah said teasingly.

"You have to date first," Kamaya said with a deep chuckle. "Are you finally dating, big brother?"

Donovan shook his head, amused by his sisters' teasing. "Don't call me Don Juan," he said, cutting an eye at Tarah.

"What's going on?" Kendrick asked, moving into the room. "Who's calling who names?"

"Tarah," Mason said, sauntering in on his brother's heels. "You don't even need to ask."

Tarah threw her brother a look. "Why do you assume I did something? How come it can't be Maitlyn or Kamaya who's doing something?"

"Because it's always you," her brothers all answered in unison.

The women laughed, Maitlyn and Kamaya nodding their heads in agreement.

Tarah rolled her eyes skyward, her arms crossing over her chest. Her lips were pushed out in a full pout as she tossed her body back against the sofa cushions.

Katherine smiled. "Y'all stop now. Donovan was just about to tell us his news."

The family all turned in Donovan's direction, eyeing him curiously. He shook his head, the attention suddenly unnerving. His brow furrowed.

"Well?" Katherine prodded. "What is it, baby?"

"I'm moving to Italy," he pronounced, his gaze sweeping around the room. "I leave at the end of the semester. I've been invited by the University of Siena in Tuscany, Italy, to come teach there. I'll be a visiting professor for one year teaching the structure of associative algebras relative to their radicals."

Tarah jumped up excitedly. "Hot dog! I get to visit Italy! Yes, yes, yes!" she exclaimed as she rushed to Donovan's side. She threw her arms around her big brother's shoulders.

"I didn't hear anyone in the room say anything about you going to Italy," their mother noted. "Sit your tail down, Tarah, and give your brother some space."

Tarah tossed her hands up as she moved back to her seat, plopping her body back down against the sofa.

Everyone in the room laughed.

Donovan laughed with them. "I hope that once I get settled, you'll all come visit me at some point," he said.

"You couldn't find a college in Texas or Florida or someplace closer? You're a mathematician, after all. Everyone needs a good numbers man," Katherine said, her bright smile dropping into a deep frown.

He shook his head, meeting his mother's gaze. His smile was consoling. "This is a great opportunity that I can't pass up. It's a definite résumé builder."

Congratulations rang warmly through the room as his siblings moved to shake his hand and give him hugs.

His mother moved to his side, her hands clasping his shoulders. There were tears in her eyes. "Why must all of you move so far away? Italy is halfway around the world, for heaven's sake!"

Senior joined them, wrapping his own arms around his wife's shoulders. "Leave that boy be. Your son's almost forty years old! Cut them apron strings already, woman!" The man's smile filled his dark face as he kissed her cheek.

She rolled her eyes, fighting the smile that pulled at her own lips and the tears that burned hot behind her eyelids. "He's only thirty-seven. He's nowhere near close to forty yet. And I'll cut the apron strings when I darn well please, Senior Boudreaux!"

Donovan smiled, the pad of his thumb swiping at a tear that had rolled down his mother's cheek. "It's not like I won't come back, Mama. I'm not planning to be there forever. And I hope you'll definitely come visit me."

Tarah suddenly waved her hands for attention. "Can I live in your apartment while you're gone?"

Senior eased his body into the queen-size bed beside his wife. Katherine sat upright against the pillows, her electronic reader open on her lap, her reading glasses perched low on her nose. She cut her eye at her husband as he snuggled his body close against hers. He leaned up on one elbow, his head resting against an open palm as he stared at her.

"What?"

"What do you mean what?"

"I mean, why are you staring at me?"

"I'm staring," he said softly, his hand trailing a heated line across her leg, "because you're so beautiful."

Katherine shifted her glasses from her face, resting them easily in her lap. She met the look the man was giving her. "What do you want, Senior Boudreaux?"

"Why do I have to want something, woman?"

"Because when you start tossing out compliments, you're up to something. So what is it?"

Senior rolled his eyes skyward as he dropped onto his side, then moved onto his back. He pulled one arm up over his head as the other clutched the covers around his body.

"I tell you how beautiful you are all the time. That doesn't mean I want something."

Katherine pulled her glasses back against her face. She threw one last gaze in his direction. "Mmm-hmm!" she muttered under her breath.

Senior laughed. "Okay, so maybe I want something," he said as he rolled back toward her.

"You're working my nerves right now, Senior," she quipped, a smile pulling at her thin lips. "You see me reading. You know I don't like to be interrupted when I'm in the middle of a good book!"

Senior shrugged his shoulders. "I was thinking that we probably need to update our wills," he said, ignoring her comment.

She pulled at her eyeglasses a second time, closing the cover on her electronic device. "What brought that up?"

"Our babies. With all of our new grandbabies we need to make sure they're going to be taken care of. We don't have much, but I want to make sure they each get a little something from us when the time comes."

Katherine nodded. "Do you remember when it was just Collin? Back then I used to think he was going to be the only grandbaby we would ever have!"

Senior laughed. "And you spoiled him like it, too!"

The matriarch nodded. "Katrina was going through so much back then, raising Collin by herself after his daddy died."

Senior fell into his thoughts, thinking about the army helicopter pilot who'd married his daughter and fathered his eldest grandson. He'd been a good man, and his untimely death during the Gulf War had been devastating. Both he and Katherine had been thrilled when Katrina had found love a second time with Matthew Stallion. Matthew loved their daughter immensely and had stepped in to parent Collin without a moment's hesitation. The couple had been blessed again when their second son, Matthew Jacoby Stallion Junior, had been born. Everyone in the family called the youngster Jake. Only his beloved grandmother called him Jacoby.

Senior tossed his wife an endearing smile. "Katrina's happy, and them boys is doing good. She and Matthew are doing a fine job raising Collin and Jake."

"My sweet little Jacoby is a handful. But he's got a great big brother!"

"Collin takes after his granddaddy," Senior said with a chuckle.

Katherine laughed with him. "That's not a bad thing! Not a bad thing at all!" She trailed a warm finger against the side of her husband's face.

"Now we've got the twins, and little Alexa, and Maitlyn will be having her little munchkin soon. Before you know it, Tarah will be married and having babies. I just think we need to make sure we're prepared."

"It used to drive me crazy worrying about our kids

getting married and having families of their own. I wanted them all to know the kind of love you and I have, but your sons were determined to do things their own way."

"And look at them now. I think my sons are doing a fine job. You were worrying for nothing."

She smiled. "I guess I was," she said as she thought about her children and the people who'd come to share their lives. Her eldest son, Mason, had married Matthew Stallion's sister, Phaedra. Mason wanted children, but Phaedra wasn't ready to rush into the responsibility. She imagined it would be another year, maybe even two before the young woman would be ready. Katherine had told her son that waiting wasn't a bad thing. It would happen when God was ready for it to happen.

Then there was Maitlyn. Her oldest daughter had been heartbroken over the demise of her first marriage despite both her parents having warned her that her ex had been no good for her. Meeting her brother's best friend, Zak Sayed, had shown Maitlyn how a woman was supposed to be treated. And now Maitlyn and Zak were expecting their first child.

With Guy and Dahlia settling in nicely with their twins, and Darryl and his wife, Camryn, loving on their new baby, only three of their children had yet to find happiness in a committed relationship. Donovan was the only son still an eligible bachelor. Their daughter Kamaya's happily-ever-after was right in front of her face, but she was the only one who couldn't see it, and their youngest, Tarah, was still looking for Mr. Right, although Tarah was often quick to settle for Mr. Right Now. Katherine blew out a low sigh.

She suddenly felt her husband eyeing her intently, and she met his stare. "I think you're worrying for nothing," she said. "Every one of our kids is doing well, and their babies will want for absolutely nothing."

Senior reached his arms around his wife's waist and hugged her close. "Maybe, but I'd rather be safe than sorry."

She nodded, gently caressing his shoulders as she hugged him back. "We've done good with our children, Senior Boudreaux," she whispered softly. "We've done really good, old man! It's time you and I both stop worrying."

"So, does that mean you're happy about Donovan going to Italy?"

"I like having my children close to home, you know that, Senior. I will never be happy about Donovan going so far away, but I'm happy that he's been blessed with this opportunity."

He gave her a quick squeeze. "Donovan needs a change of scenery. This trip will be good for him. He's been focused on school and work and nothing else for too long now."

Katherine blew a soft sigh. "Maybe, but I'm still gonna miss my baby!"

Senior laughed heartily. "Your babies are grown!" he said as he reached to swipe a tear from her eye.

She leaned her cheek into the palm of his hand. "They will always be my babies!"

Senior reached up to kiss her mouth, allowing his lips

to linger against hers for a good long while. Katherine broke the connection, suddenly laughing as she turned off her reader and rested it against the nightstand. She reached to turn off the light that decorated the tabletop.

Her husband eyed the wide grin across her face. "What's so funny?"

"I think we should make a baby!" she said, still giggling as she nestled herself beneath him.

Senior laughed with her. "You're hoping for a miracle, aren't you?"

"Not really. I just thought we could have a whole lot of fun practicing," she answered as she slid her lips back to his.

Chapter 2

Donovan moved from his kitchen into his family room, hanging up the telephone he carried in his hand. He'd been on a conference call with Maitlyn and his brothers, acquiring help for his impending trip. His Lafayette Street loft had been his single greatest investment, and he needed to ensure that someone in the family stayed on top of things while he was gone, lest Tarah turn his home into a sorority party house.

Making sure the doors were locked and the security system engaged, he headed to his office. He sat down in the leather executive's chair, pulling it up to the large oak desk as he turned on his computer. As he waited for it to power on, Donovan folded his hands in his lap, dropping into deep thought.

Donovan was the third child and the second son in

the family of nine. With a doctorate in mathematics, he was a tenured professor at Tulane University. The most conservative of all his siblings, he was an intellectual challenge to most. His staid demeanor made his sister Katrina, a district court judge, and his brother Mason, a billionaire entrepreneur and business executive, look wild in comparison. His younger siblings frequently professed that he defied all logic with them having careers in the arts and him having no artistic inclinations whatsoever. Even his brother Kendrick, who had often kept much of his life a deep, dark secret until meeting Vanessa, was more outspoken and outgoing than Donovan tended to be.

But Donovan had secrets, too, the likes of which would make his whole family sit up and take notice. His very conservative, very organized lifestyle had always been an open book, and now he was keeping details close to the vest. His interest in Italy was just the tip of the cache of secrets he'd been keeping from his family. A full grin pulled wide across his face.

He focused on the lengthy list of email messages that filled his inbox folder. He was searching for one in particular, and when he found the familiar email address his smile widened.

For months now he'd been pen pals with a woman who lived in Italy. A woman he had yet to meet or speak to in person. He only knew her from the award-winning books she was renowned for, her promotional photo gracing the back cover of each. But he'd become obsessed with the email messages from her that came daily, the engaging exchanges brightening his otherwise

dull existence. And now he was being afforded an opportunity to visit Italy and meet her in person. Never
much of a risk taker, Donovan rarely found himself
out of his comfort zone. He could only begin to imagine what his siblings would have to say if any of them
were to find out.

He didn't have to imagine what his parents would
say. He could already hear their admonishments and
concerns, both asking questions he didn't necessarily
have answers for. He had never heard of any online relationship turning out well. For all any of them knew,
he could have just as easily been chatting with Bubba in
the state penitentiary. He no more knew who was on the
other end of that computer than she did. He only knew
what he was being told, and any of it could have been
a bold-faced lie. The anonymity of the internet made
embellishing and stretching the truth an easy thing to
do. But something about the eloquence of her words had
Donovan trusting that he did indeed have a connection
with the illustrious author.

He read the message that had come hours earlier.

I live a charmed life. I get to live in a beautiful villa in
the Tuscan Maremma, eat pasta prepared by an amazing Italian chef and travel to charming cities whenever I
want. What's not to love? I imagine that finally meeting
you will be the icing on some very sweet, sweet cake!
So, please, come. I can't wait to show you everything
exquisite about Italy.

A shiver of excitement surged up Donovan's spine.
He reached for the four-hundred-page mystery novel

that rested on the corner of the desk. *Mayhem and Madness* by Gianna Martelli had landed on the *New York Times* bestseller list three weeks earlier and didn't seem to be going anyplace anytime soon. He flipped the book in his hand to stare at the photograph on the back jacket.

Gianna Martelli was a stunning beauty, and he imagined that the professionally shot black-and-white image didn't begin to do her justice. Her dark eyes were focused on the camera, and he felt as if she were staring directly at him. The look she was giving was searing, her gaze intense. But there was something about her expression that gave him pause, made him wish he could reach through the pages to draw her into his arms and hold her tight. He sighed.

Two books ago he'd reached out to email her, wanting to offer his opinion of her current novel at the time. He'd been excited to share his opinions about her characters, the protagonist a math professor at a historically black college. He'd been eager to tell her where she'd gotten it wrong and what had been wholeheartedly right. He had only half expected a polite but scripted response. Instead, he'd gotten an intriguingly worded reply that had challenged his sensibilities. Curiosity had gotten the best of him and he'd written back, receiving another reply that had him suddenly wanting more. Before he knew it, they were exchanging lengthy emails and a delightful friendship was born.

He typed a quick message back.

You've convinced me and now I'm counting the days. I can't wait to see that sunset you are always bragging about.

After adding his travel details, he pushed the send button. Moving from his office to his bedroom, he pulled an oversize suitcase from a closet shelf and began to pack.

Rushing into the large kitchen, Carina looked from her husband to her father and back. Both men paused, concern washing over their expressions.

"What's wrong?" Graham questioned.

"Are you okay?" Franco asked, resting the knife in his hand on the butcher-block counter.

She shook her head vehemently. "Gianna's going to kill me!"

The two men cut eyes at each other.

"What did you do, Carina?" Franco asked, eyeing his daughter with a narrowed gaze.

She raised both hands. "It's really not that bad, but Gianna isn't going to like it!" she exclaimed.

"What isn't she going to like?" Graham asked.

Carina crossed the room to stare out a window. She moved from one to the other, and then to the door, to ensure that her twin was nowhere near.

Franco shook his head. "Gianna went into town for me. She's not here."

"He's coming to Italy," Carina blurted. "He'll be here next week."

"Who's coming to Italy?"

"Donovan Boudreaux, the math professor from the United States."

Both men seemed confused, tossing each other another look.

Carina sighed. "The man she's been communicating with, except she doesn't know she's been communicating with him because I've been sending the messages."

Both men snapped in unison. "You've been doing what?"

The young woman nodded. "I've been pretending to be Gianna. He's been writing to her, and I've been answering."

"Carina, why would you do something like that?" Graham snapped.

"Because I knew she wouldn't, and I think they would make a really great couple. He's just as nerdy as she is."

"But he hasn't been building a relationship with your sister, Carina—he's been building one with you," Franco said, crossing his arms over his chest.

Carina shook her head. "That's not true. Every word I sent, she wrote. I copied them out of her journals."

"You read your sister's journals?" Her father's look was disapproving.

"I've been reading her journals since we were twelve. Besides, I am her personal assistant. I'm supposed to answer her mail."

"I don't think that's what your sister intended, daughter." Franco shook his head from side to side. He went back to chopping the bulb of garlic that rested on the wooden chopping board. "Gianna is going to kill you!"

Graham laughed. "She is definitely going to kill you," he said.

Carina rolled her eyes at her husband. "Thanks for the support."

"So, what do you know about this guy?" Graham asked. "How do you know he's not a psycho?"

"He teaches at Tulane University in New Orleans. He comes from a big family, and he reads the same boring stuff Gianna reads."

"So he is a psycho!"

"He's very sweet and a bit of a romantic. He's exactly what Gianna needs."

"So, tell me," Graham said, turning to stare at his wife, a wooden spoon waving in his hand, "exactly when were you going to tell Gianna about this guy?"

"I hadn't figured that out. I thought I had a little more time until he decided to come to Italy to meet me... I mean her."

Graham continued to eyeball her. "I'm having some issues with this," he said. "You've been having a relationship with another man for weeks..."

"Months actually," Carina interrupted, her tone casual.

Graham paused, his eyebrows raised. "Months?"

His wife nodded as she gave him a quick shrug. "I was building a friendship between them. That takes time. And I was going to tell her. I think."

He shook his head. "You've been building this relationship for months now, but I'm supposed to believe that you did it for your sister, when you didn't even know if you were going to tell her?"

"You're making it sound worse than it is!"

"It sounds the way it sounds, Carina, and it's not kosher! It's not kosher at all!"

Her father moved from the tomato sauce he'd put on

the stove toward the door. "I'll let you two have a minute," he said. "Watch my pot while I'm gone, please."

Carina blew out a soft sigh. She locked gazes with her husband, noting the disappointment and confusion that gleamed from his eyes. She didn't have the words to explain how she'd rationalized what she'd done. All she knew was that in the beginning, it had made all the sense in the world to her. And that even in that moment she knew beyond any doubt that she'd done the right thing.

Since the publication of Gianna's first book, Carina had stepped in to do those things Gianna neglected to do for herself. From managing her fan page to answering reader questions, Carina had been her sister's personal assistant and marketing guru, maintaining her Twitter, Facebook and Instagram accounts. When Donovan's first email message had come, there had been something in the tone of his words that had caught her attention. His comments had been thoughtful and provoking, his words laden with emotion. She instinctively knew he was exactly what her best friend in the whole wide world needed.

Her response had been all Gianna, the wisecracking, tongue-in-cheek retorts her sister was known for. As their emails had gotten lengthier, she'd pulled lines and paragraphs from Gianna's personal writings to respond, wanting him to know her twin the way she knew her, in her sister's own words. And it had worked because now he wanted to meet the woman he'd befriended. Admittedly, Carina hadn't thought her plan through to the end. She'd imagined that once she'd vetted the man, she could have told Gianna and passed on the reins. Despite hoping that her twin would be happy to step in and take over, Carina knew that happy was probably going to be the last thing Gianna would feel about the situation.

She felt her husband still staring at her, and she lifted her eyes back to his. "Donovan likes Gianna. Everything he knows, he knows about Gianna. He doesn't know me or anything about me! And when she finds out and gets to know him, she's going to like him, too. I'd bet my last dollar on it. I just wanted her to be as happy as you and I are, and you know she wouldn't have done anything like this on her own."

Graham shook his head from side to side. "So when do you plan to tell Gianna?"

"Tell Gianna what?" Gianna asked as she moved into the room. She looked from one to the other. "What's going on?"

Carina moved too quickly to her husband's side, leaning against him for support. The two exchanged a quick look, a wave of nervous energy palpable around them.

Moving to the counter, Gianna dropped her bags against the wooden top. Her eyes were still locked on her sister and brother-in-law. The bubbling pot on the stove interrupted the moment as tomato sauce suddenly spewed over the sides and down to the stove top.

"Oh, hell!" Carina exclaimed, moving to lower the heat on their father's meal.

Gianna watched with one hand on her hip as she waited for the duo to clean the mess. When the last dishrag had been rinsed, the pot back on simmer, she asked a second time, "So what is it that you have to tell me?"

Mumbling, Graham leaned over to kiss his wife's cheek, then moved toward the door. Without another word, he disappeared through the entrance, leaving the two women alone. Gianna moved to stand in front of her sister, her arms crossed over her chest.

"What's going on, Sissy?"

"Why don't we sit down? Did you find everything you needed at the market?"

Gianna shook her head, her index finger waving in front of her sister's face. "Oh, no, you don't! You are not changing the subject, and don't you move until you answer my question!"

Carina took a deep breath and then another. "I found you a boyfriend," she said, and then she spewed out the story, not bothering to take another inhale of air until the last word had spilled past her lips.

"Open the door, Gianna," Franco commanded. "You can't hide in there forever."

"I'm not hiding!" Gianna yelled back. "I just don't want to talk to anyone."

"Now, daughter! And don't make me say it again."

Gianna sighed deeply as she moved onto her feet toward her office door. She undid the lock and pulled it open just enough to peer out into the hallway. Standing on the other side, her father gave her that look, his mouth pursed tightly, his eyes narrowed. Sighing again, she stepped aside to let the man enter.

Franco moved to the upholstered sofa and sat down,

turning his gaze to stare at his daughter. Neither spoke, Gianna still pouting in anger. As she sat down beside him, she couldn't help but marvel at her father. His calm demeanor was soothing, and his dashing good looks made her smile.

The older she and her sister got, the more Gianna thought they were starting to look like their beloved father. His complexion was warm, his loose curls more silver than black. They had his nose and jawline, but neither had inherited his chilling blue eyes. He swore that both his girls resembled their mother, but Gianna didn't necessarily agree, thinking they were a nice mesh of the two. She suddenly thought about her mother.

The beautiful black woman from New York City had been the love of her father's life. A chance meeting while Angela Wilson had been an exchange student in Tuscany had solidified their future. Franco had always believed that they would have grown old together, but his beloved Angela had suffered a brain aneurysm when the twins were twelve years old. The loss had been devastating. Franco had thrown himself into running his family winery and loving his children. He still mourned the loss.

As long as Gianna could remember, she and her sister's antics had been enough to keep him on his toes, and keep his head gray. And despite their love for one another, they spent more time angry with each other than not angry, with Gianna, the elder by ten minutes, always pouting because of something Carina had done.

"So when do you plan to speak to your sister?" her father asked.

Gianna rolled her eyes skyward. "Never! I cannot believe she would do this to me."

"It was a little extreme, but her heart was in the right place."

"This man is coming to visit, and he thinks there's something between us and there isn't. I don't know anything about him."

Her father nodded. "I imagine he's going to be disappointed."

"And his disappointment falls on me. She used my name. That's unforgiveable."

"Everything is forgivable."

"Not this."

Franco chuckled softly. "Even this. You just need to figure out how to make it right."

"Why do I need to make it right? I didn't do anything!"

"That may be true, but just like you pointed out, your sister used your name and now a man who doesn't deserve it is going to be disappointed."

Gianna screamed as she shook two fists in the air. "Aargh! I swear I could kill her!" She began to rant in her native Italian.

Franco chuckled softly. "That's an option," he said with a nod, "but I'm sure you can come up with something more creative. Something that will make everybody happy." He tapped a warm palm against her knee.

Gianna shook her head as her father stood back on his feet.

"Carina loves you, Gianna. And you love her. What

she did, she did out of love. Don't you forget that, *mia cara*." He leaned down to kiss her cheek.

She nodded slowly, meeting his gaze. *"Va bene, papà,"* she said, her expression unmoved.

As the patriarch made his way out of the room, Gianna rose to lock the door behind him. She wasn't yet ready to face her twin, and she knew it would only take a quick minute for Carina to come busting her way inside if she found an opportunity.

She moved back to her desk and the oversize manila folder that rested on its surface. After her admission Carina had given it to Gianna, insisting she read the contents. Gianna still hadn't bothered to break the cover to see just how deep Carina's deception ran.

There was a soft knock at the office door. Carina called her name but Gianna ignored her sister, still staring at the stack of documents. Despite her anger she was intrigued, the curiosity pulling at her. Of all the stunts her sister had pulled over the years, this one had to be her most devious by far. And she was scared to death, fearful that there might be something she liked hidden in those pages that would draw her into her twin sister's madness.

Outside Gianna's window, a plethora of bright stars and a full moon illuminated the dark sky. She'd been reading for hours, the home on the other side of the office door having gone quiet for the night. Carina had tried more than once to get her attention until she'd finally given up, her tear-filled tone apologizing again and again for what she'd done.

Gianna picked up the very first message from the man named Donovan, rereading the words she'd already read a few dozen times.

Dear Ms. Martelli,
My name is Donovan Boudreaux. I'm a math professor at Tulane University in New Orleans, Louisiana. I have been a fan of yours since your first book, *Bruised and Battered*. Despite my previous intentions to write and tell you how much I've enjoyed your writing, I've always stopped myself, feeling that you probably would not want to be inundated with more fan mail. But I was so enthralled with your last story, and the character Dr. Hanover, that I could not let the opportunity to tell you what I think pass by. Your artistry is rare and your words are epic. I was captivated from the first sentence to the last. However, I'm curious to know if you intentionally wanted your readers to empathize with the protagonist despite his being so unlikable. Your disdain for this man was obvious, but as I found myself rooting for him I had to question your intent and wondered if the reflection of him as a man mirrored my own projections. Or are they reflections you masterfully and purposely elicited from us? I'd love to discuss him in further detail. I do hope you'll respond.
Yours truly,
Donovan Boudreaux

Carina's response had been brilliant, her sister pulling excerpts from two news interviews she'd done and quoting one of her favorite proverbs.

Mr. Boudreaux,

Thank you for your kind words. Your support of my work is appreciated, and I found your question interesting. I think what you deemed disdain was anything but. Dr. Hanover was one of my favorite characters to write, and I'm pleased that the dynamics of his personality did not get lost in the details of the mystery. Dr. Hanover's character was drawn to invoke a whirlwind of emotion from the reader, that connection both thought-provoking and substantive. To quote one of my favorite Scriptures: "As iron sharpens iron, so one person sharpens another." Proverbs 27:17. Dr. Hanover served his purpose if you were rooting for him, his advice and wisdom intended to sharpen yours. Thank you for reaching out and please do keep in touch.

Happy reading,

Gianna

And Donovan had kept in touch, continuing to write. His brief paragraphs had expanded to lengthier messages, and Carina had kept up nicely, pulling her responses right from Gianna's private writings. Gianna was surprised by how her twin had pieced the responses together, some of the replies so spot-on that she would never have believed Carina had anything at all to do with them if she hadn't known better. It was almost as if her twin had been stowed away in her head, privy to her thoughts and possessing an understanding of her worldview. It was a cosmic connection like no other, and Gianna didn't know if she could have done the same so successfully.

She pulled one of his last messages from the folder, the literary connection having evolved into something she couldn't even begin to define.

Dearest Gianna,
I marvel at how you're able to articulate what I'm feeling, when I can't even find the words. You are correct. I would be disappointed if I'm not selected for this teaching fellowship. But I'm a man, and my disappointment should not be telling. There are some issues I should not be sensitive about, and because I'm a man that sensitivity should definitely not show. If it does, it would be seen as a sign of weakness. What woman would want a weak man?

Gianna marveled, too. Her sister's crafted reply had been award-worthy.

Donovan, Donovan, Donovan!
Every woman wants a man who owns his feelings! Sensitivity can never be seen as weakness if it walks hand in hand with honesty. Owning our emotions is empowering. Of course you'll be disappointed! You worked hard to qualify for the opportunity. You want it! You are deserving of it! So claim it and think of the day you land in Italy, when you can stand beneath the brightest blue sky and watch the sunset that I watch daily. No woman should want a man who would do any less than that!

And now this stranger, who was connected with Gianna in a way that she found outrageously absurd, was on his way to the Italian coast, expecting that she would be as excited to see him as he was to see her. It was crazy and overwhelming, and despite every ounce of reservation she was feeling, she was intrigued and curious in the same breath.

Chapter 3

Donovan stood with his brother Kendrick, the two men waiting in the flight hangar for the preflight maintenance check on their brother Mason's private plane to be completed. Membership having its privileges surely applied as Donovan eyed the luxury aircraft, one of a dozen planes that Mason had at his disposal. The opportunity to fly private planes had been a gift, the gesture humbling, and Donovan couldn't begin to know how he'd ever be able to repay the favor.

"I promise, baby! I will call you the minute I land," Kendrick was saying while rolling his eyes. He exchanged a look with his brother as he continued his conversation. "Vanessa! It's only three days. I'll be back before you know it. I promise!"

There was a pause, Vanessa's raised voice echoing

out of the receiver in Kendrick's hand. The man blew a heavy sigh. "I swear, honey! This is not a covert mission. I am not disappearing underground on any assignment. I ride a desk now, remember?"

Donovan smiled. Kendrick settling down with his new wife had come with a host of challenges for his younger brother. The couple had met when the FBI agent had been assigned to Vanessa's protective detail, whisking her away to one of the world's most romantic honeymoon spots to protect their cover. Despite Kendrick's assurances that his secret agent days were over, Vanessa remained unconvinced, crippled by anxiety every time he disappeared from town.

Kendrick shook his head as he disconnected. "She's going to kill me."

Donovan laughed. "You tagging along with me isn't what she thinks it is, is it?"

Kendrick shook his head. "I have some work to take care of once we drop you off and send Mason's plane back his way. I'll be meeting up with my unit in Florence and going on to Greece. I just didn't give Vanessa *all* the details of this little venture. I just told her you were scared and wanted me to check things out for you."

"Why would I be scared?"

His brother shrugged. "Your sisters have her convinced that you're a little soft. I just rolled with it."

Donovan's eyes widened as he stared his brother down.

"What?" Kendrick asked, tossing him a look. "Even you know the girls think you're a little easy. They're always afraid someone's going to take advantage of you because you're so trusting."

Donovan shook his head.

Kendrick chuckled. "Hey, it's no big deal. It gives me an excuse to go do what I need to do."

"Do I even want to ask?" Donovan said.

"Nope! Because if I tell you I'll have to shoot you, and we don't want to ruin your trip." Kendrick laughed as he changed the subject. "So, are you excited?"

"I'm nervous. *Not* scared," he emphasized, "but nervous."

"About teaching? That's your thing, bro! Why would you be nervous?"

Donovan met his brother's curious stare. "I just… well…" he stammered, his eyes skating back and forth as he tried to choose his words carefully. "There's someone…a woman… She…"

Kendrick eyed him with a raised brow. "Okay, spill it. What aren't you telling me?"

There was a moment of pause before Donovan answered, lost in his thoughts about Gianna as he reflected on what he knew about the woman.

From her bio, he'd discovered that she held two advanced degrees in science and mathematics. From their communications, he knew that she abhorred traditional intellectual attitudes. So much so that she'd been initially reluctant to communicate with him when she discovered he was a professor.

From reading her novels, he knew that she was proficient at spinning a good thriller and murder mystery. Gianna had a talent for creating male protagonists who appealed to male readers. Despite her literary accolades, she was famously reclusive and purposely avoided the public eye, preferring to spend her time at her family's Tuscan estate working in their winery.

From their exchanges, he took her to be something of a free spirit who practiced yoga religiously, followed an organic diet and was a self-professed nudist. She was passionate about the family's Tuscan estate and winery, and had once stated that she would readily give up her pursuit of the next great novel to work the vineyards.

He took a deep breath. "I have a friend there, and I'm nervous about meeting her," he said finally. "We've only communicated by email."

Kendrick grinned, his smile full and bright. "A friend? When did you get a friend? Who's a girl? In Italy?" he questioned, crossing his arms over his chest.

Donovan felt his own grin spread full and wide across his face. "We've been acquainted for a while now."

"And she's Italian?"

Donovan nodded.

"Is she in education, too?"

"She's a writer. Her name is Gianna."

Kendrick paused for a moment. "Gianna Martelli? The author of *Mayhem and Madness*?"

"You know her?"

"I know her writing. Vanessa bought me a copy of her book to read. It's really good."

"She's extremely talented," Donovan stated.

"She's also quite the looker, if I remember correctly," Kendrick noted with a nod.

Donovan shrugged. "She's all right," he said, trying to keep his tone in check.

Kendrick gave him a swift punch to his upper arm. "Look at you, big brother! I think you're actually blushing! Wait until I tell the family!"

Donovan laughed, lifting his hands up as if in surrender. "You wouldn't. You cannot tell the girls! I would never live it down." He mocked his sisters, imitating Tarah's shrill tone. "Don Juan has a girlfriend? Don Juan is actually speaking to a woman? Let's give Don Juan some advice!"

Kendrick laughed heartily. "You're right. I can't do that to you!"

"Thank you!" He changed the subject. "So have you and Vanessa decided on a honeymoon spot yet?"

As the two men continued their conversation, the flight attendant gestured for their attention. "Gentlemen, we're ready for you to board now," the woman said politely. She gave them both a smile, her gaze shifting between them.

Donovan reached for his carry-on bag and led the way. Minutes later the two men sat comfortably, secured in the plush leather seats as the plane taxied down the runway. He relished the camaraderie he shared with his siblings. He could laugh easily with his brothers, and since it wasn't often that the two were able to spend time together, he was grateful that Kendrick was taking the trip with him, whatever the other man's reasons.

Donovan also didn't mind the teasing from any of his family. He knew that no matter what, he had their support, and the tight bond they all shared was unconditional. But as he thought about Gianna and what might be waiting for him when they finally landed, he was only willing to share so much about the exquisite woman and what he felt about their unique situation. As he stared out the window, watching as the plane lifted easily into the cloud-filled sky, Donovan took a deep breath and then another, hoping that the fear he felt in his heart didn't show on his face.

Sophie Mugabe and Alessandra Donati stood at the arrival gate of Pisa International Airport waiting for the American professor to gather his luggage and exit the travel center. Both were excited as they stood with handmade signs, Donovan's name printed in bold black letters across both sides.

Sophie was Donovan's host and the department chair at the University of Siena. She'd been following him since they'd first met three years earlier at the International Conference on Mathematics and Statistics. That year the conference had been held in London, and Donovan had been presenting the theories he'd published in his book, *The Deconstruction of Associative Algebras of Prime Characteristic.*

Sophie had been enamored from day one, her enthusiasm for the professor and his work almost compulsive. Her regular emails had been just shy of stalking, but he'd been exceptionally kind in his responses. The prospect of getting to know him personally through the next year had her excited in a way she would have never imagined. She was fighting to contain the emotion bubbling through her midsection, desperate to maintain her decorum in front of her student.

Alessandra Donati stood with indifference, her gaze sweeping around the airport lobby. Since the girl's freshman year, Professor Mugabe had mistaken her proficiency with mathematics for interest, singling her out for attention that Alessandra had neither needed nor wanted. But the perks of being the teacher's pet outweighed the disadvantages. So despite wanting to be in Venice with her friends who'd driven up for the day, she'd agreed to come with her mentor to welcome some visiting professor from the United States. She sighed heavily as she looked down at the thin gold watch on her wrist.

"He's landed," Sophie said, excitement ringing in her tone. "It should not be too much longer now."

Alessandra forced a smile onto her face. She was about to comment when she caught sight of the college professor, the man eyeing them both curiously. The distinguished black man smiled sweetly, and the gesture took her breath away. Tall, dark and handsome to the nth degree, he actually had her heartbeat fluttering. She threw her teacher a quick look, not missing the other woman's glazed stare. Her professor was likewise moved.

"He's quite handsome, isn't he?" Sophie muttered as she waved excitedly.

Alessandra chuckled beneath her breath. "Oh, yes, he is!" she exclaimed.

"Professor Mugabe! What a surprise!" Donovan said,

moving to their side. He leaned in to give his benefactor a warm embrace.

"Dr. Boudreaux, welcome to Italy! I could not let you arrive and not be here personally to welcome you. I hope that your trip was pleasant?"

Donovan nodded. "The flight was great. My brother flew with me, and it gave us an opportunity to catch up."

Sophie tossed a look over his shoulder, her eyes skating back and forth. "Your brother is with you?"

Donovan smiled again. "He's actually headed on to Greece as soon as they refuel his plane."

Alessandra cleared her throat, stepping forward for attention. Her eyes swept from one to the other, settling on the beautiful black man.

Sophie tapped her hand to her forehead. "Forgive me. Where are my manners! Dr. Boudreaux, allow me to introduce you to one of our prized students. This is Alessandra Donati. Alessandra is a senior mathematics major. She's quite gifted and looking forward to being in your class this semester."

Alessandra smiled, her gaze narrowing ever so slightly. "Dr. Boudreaux, it's very nice to meet you," she said as she tossed the length of her blond hair over her shoulder. She extended a manicured hand in his direction as she batted her false eyelashes.

"The pleasure is mine, Ms. Donati," he said, shaking her hand.

"I was very excited to hear that you would be coming to the university. Your paper on Lie algebras was quite engaging."

Donovan laughed. "It really wasn't, but I appreciate you saying so."

The young woman's smile was bright, the glint in her eye even brighter.

Sophie interrupted the moment. "I thought we'd get you settled into your cottage, then take you by the school and out for your first meal here in Italy. Unless you have other plans?"

Donovan took a deep breath. "I'd actually love to visit the school, but I'm having dinner with friends. I apologize, I didn't know..."

She shook her head swiftly, interrupting his comment. "Oh, please, no apology necessary. I just thought I'd make the offer."

"You have friends here in Tuscany?" Alessandra asked.

Donovan smiled. "Yes, Gianna Martelli and the Martelli family. They have a vineyard in the heart of the Tuscan Maremma, not far from the province of Grosseto."

Both women shrugged indifferently. "Martelli is a very common name here in Italy," Sophie said, disappointment shimmering in her tone.

Donovan nodded. "Perhaps we can have breakfast in the morning and you can show me around? I'm very excited to see the campus and get acquainted with the faculty."

The older woman grinned. "Definitely! That is definitely doable."

Gianna was as nervous as her sister, the two women scurrying about trying to ensure everything was perfect before Donovan Boudreaux arrived for dinner. Freshly cut flowers decorated the home, resting atop the tables and counters. All the windows had been opened, and a warm breeze blew like a whisper through the space. A roasted chicken scented the air, and handmade pasta waited on the wooden countertop to be dropped into lightly salted water.

Franco and Graham exchanged a look as both women came to an abrupt halt, eyeing each other from across the room. A silent conversation passed between them, something unique that only they understood. The brevity of it could have filled a thimble, but in that brief moment there was something magnanimous that happened between them.

Gianna sighed softly, and as if she'd caught the warm breath, Carina folded her hand into a tight fist, pulling it to the spot between her breasts. Both women smiled, and then just as abruptly resumed their frantic fussing about.

Franco broke the silence. "Have you spoken to this man, Gianna?" he asked curiously.

She paused to meet her father's stare. "I sent him a text message. His flight should have landed by now, and once he gets settled he's going to find his way here."

"Did you want me to go get him?" Graham asked.

"No!" both women answered in unison.

"It's just a ride!" Graham replied, bristling slightly.

"You would tell him. I know you," Carina said.

Gianna nodded in agreement. "It has to come from us. From Carina."

"Why from me?" her sister asked, turning to stare at Gianna.

"Because this is all your fault. You're the one who allowed this lie to snowball."

"You could have told him already," Carina said. "You've been emailing back and forth for the last two weeks. So you've been playing in that snow, too!"

"I could have," Gianna said matter-of-factly. "But then he might not have come." She cut an eye in Carina's direction.

Her sister laughed. "I knew you would like him!"

"I find him interesting. So, yes, I'm curious."

Carina jumped up and down excitedly. "You *really* like him!" she exclaimed.

Franco laughed as he rose from his seat, peering out the front window. "That's a good thing because your new friend just pulled up outside!"

Chapter 4

Donovan stood nervously outside the luxury villa. After settling into the one bedroom cottage the university had rented for him for the next year, he'd asked the property owner for directions to the winery. The rotund woman looked like soft biscuit dough and spoke little if any English. She had stared at him, chattering away in Italian, and despite the obvious communication issues, he'd felt right at home. It had taken a moment, but she'd eventually pointed him in the direction of the groundskeeper, who spoke perfect English and had been happy to give him a ride.

Donovan had read the winery's promotional brochures, scouring their website for anything he could learn. Cantina Moderna was a restored country farmhouse situated on a luxurious hilltop. It was surrounded by vineyards and olive groves, and the views were breathtaking. He knew from his readings that the entire wine estate included the vineyards, a state-of-the-art wine cellar and the private villa.

The *bottaia*, or wine cellar, was modern, yet sat in perfect harmony with the surrounding landscape. It showcased massive, hand-hewn oak barrels that held aged and refined wine. There was a meeting room that looked out to the Ombrone Valley and could host up to sixty people, and a tasting room with panoramic views equipped with one hundred indoor seats and a professional, gourmet kitchen. There were also rooms for the actual wine-making and a warehouse that had been designed to carry out the production needs of the winery from wine-making to bottling.

Now, standing at the edge of the floral beds that bordered the stunning home and wine facility, Donovan found himself feeling like a teen on his first date, anxiety flooding every muscle in his body. In one hand, he held a stunning bouquet of orange and pink roses, lisianthus, orchids and vibrant green ruscus tied with a simple yellow ribbon. In the other, he clutched a bottle of homemade strawberry vinaigrette, courtesy of his landlady, because how could you bring wine to a family with their own winery? He took a deep breath, and then a second one before moving slowly toward the entrance to knock on the front door.

Donovan was just about to knock a second time when Franco Martelli swung open the door, greeting him cheerily. The man pumped his arm enthusiastically as the two shook hands. "*Benvenuto*, Dr. Boudreaux!" he said as he pulled him inside the home, the door closing easily behind them.

Donovan smiled. "*Buonasera*, Signor Martelli. Thank you for having me in your home."

"Please, call me Franco." The patriarch gestured around the room. "Let me introduce you," he said as he pointed to a man sitting on a stool at an oversize counter. "This is my son-in-law, Graham Porter. Graham is married to my daughter Carina."

Graham came to his feet, extending his hand in greeting. "It's nice to meet you," he said, eyeing Donovan with reservation.

Donovan nodded. "The pleasure is mine. Gianna has told me a lot about you. She holds you in very high regard."

Graham smiled ever so slightly as he and Franco exchanged a look. "The girls should be out in a moment," he said. "You know how women do. It takes forever to make sure their faces are just right."

Donovan nodded his understanding. "I have four sisters. I understand perfectly."

"If you are like my husband and my father, then I'm sure you exaggerate," a warm voice chimed from the other side of the room. "We really are not that bad."

Donovan turned, his eyes skipping anxiously in the direction of the voice. He was greeted by a bright smile, the young woman moving quickly to his side. "Donovan, hello. I'm Carina Martelli-Porter. Gianna's sister. Welcome!"

"Carina, hello!"

"How was your trip?"

His head continued to bob up and down. "It was good. Very good. Thank you for asking."

Carina moved to her husband's side. An awkward silence suddenly filled the space, the family watching Donovan anxiously. They all seemed to take a collective breath, heavy sighs blowing around the room.

Carina pressed a palm to her husband's chest. "Darling, pour Dr. Boudreaux a glass of wine!" she said, her voice quivering ever so slightly. She shifted her gaze in Donovan's direction.

"Dr. Boudreaux, please, have a seat!" she said as she gestured toward the couch with her hand.

"Thank you, and please, call me Donovan."

He suddenly remembered the bottle in his hand. "This is for the family. It's…"

Carina interrupted. "Strawberry vinaigrette! You must be staying with Signora Rossi."

He smiled. "I am. How did you know?"

Carina held up the bottle he'd passed to her. "This stuff is pure gold and hard to come by. I'd recognize it anywhere. We are always trying to copy her recipe, and no one in the village has ever been able to get it right!"

Graham handed Donovan a full goblet of red wine as he took a seat in an upholstered chair, the floral bouquet resting in his lap. Carina moved to the chair across from him.

"I guess there really is no easy way to say this," she started.

Donovan eyed her curiously. "To say what?"

Her eyes flitted between the men in the room, pausing momentarily over each one of them. "There's something I need to tell you."

"Are you boring my company with one of your stories about me, Sissy?" another female voice interjected.

Everyone in the room turned at the same time. Gianna Martelli stood in the doorway, a bright smile painting her expression. Donovan pushed himself up from his seat, a wave of anxiety washing over him. Gianna met his stare, a nervous twitch pulsing at the edge of her lip. Light danced in her eyes as her gaze shifted from the top of his head to the floor beneath his feet and back, finally setting on his face.

Donovan Boudreaux was neatly attired, wearing a casual summer suit in tan-colored linen with a white dress shirt open at the collar. Brown leather loafers completed his look. His dark hair was cropped low and close, and he sported just the faintest hint of a goatee. His features were chiseled, and at first glance she could have easily mistaken him for a high-fashion model. Nothing about him screamed teacher. The man was drop-dead gorgeous, and as she stared, he took her breath away.

The moment was suddenly surreal, as though everything was moving in slow motion. As she glided to his side, Donovan was awed by the sheer magnitude of the moment, feeling as if he was lost somewhere deep in the sweetest dream. And then she touched him, her slender arms reaching around to give him a warm hug.

"It's nice to finally meet you," Gianna said softly. "Welcome to Italy."

Donovan's smile spread full across his face, his gaze dancing over her features. Although she and her sister were identical, he would have easily proclaimed Gianna the most beautiful woman he'd ever laid eyes on. The photo on the dust jacket of her books didn't begin to do her justice. Her complexion was dark honey, a sun-kissed glow emanating from unblemished skin. Her eyes were large saucers, blue-black in color and reminded him of vast expanses of black ice. Her features were delicate, a button nose and thin lips framed by lush, thick waves of jet-black hair that fell to midwaist on a petite frame. She was tiny, almost fragile, but carried herself as though she stood inches taller. She wore a floral-print, ankle-length skirt and a simple white shirt that stopped just below her small bustline, exposing a washboard stomach. Gianna Martelli was stunning!

Starstruck, Donovan suddenly realized he hadn't spoken, standing with his mouth open in awe. He swallowed hard as he took a deep inhale of air.

"Gianna, hello!" he finally exclaimed, unable to contain the excitement in his voice. He suddenly remembered the flowers he was still clutching, and thrusted them at her. "These are for you," he said.

She grinned as she pressed her nose into the bouquet, taking a deep inhale of their sweet aroma. "They're beautiful. Thank you," she said politely.

The two stood face-to-face, nervous energy like a match and lighter fluid igniting the space between them. Their gazes danced back and forth together, both taking in the moment.

"I hope everyone's hungry," Franco interrupted as he lifted the lid on a pot bubbling with salted water.

Everyone turned to watch as he added in a bowlful of homemade ravioli. "These won't take any time at all."

Gianna reached for Donovan's hand. "Help me put these in water while we chat," she said.

She suddenly peppered him with questions about himself and his family. In the blink of an eye everyone's anxiety dissipated, the five of them chatting and laughing easily together.

"So, tell us about your work," Franco said as he reached for the large wooden bowl filled with tossed salad.

"There's really not much to tell," Donovan said as he pressed a cloth napkin to his full lips and rested it back in his lap. "I teach and I love it. I'm excited to have this particular opportunity. This year I'll be teaching advanced mathematics at the university."

Gianna waved her hand. "Donovan is being modest. He's quite accomplished in his field. He's held membership in several professional organizations, served on a number of science and technology boards, and he's received numerous awards not only for his work and knowledge in the field of mathematics, but for his community service, as well."

She tossed him a bright smile and he smiled back, impressed that she remembered so much about him.

"Where did you get your degree?" Graham asked, just before taking a bite of his ravioli.

"I did my graduate work at MIT."

Graham nodded. "Very impressive. I attended Oxford. That's where I met Carina and Gianna."

"I always hated math when I was in school," Carina interjected. "Numbers are always so boring."

"Not really," Donovan said. "Numbers are extremely complex, and there are a myriad of ways to get them from point A to point B. The excitement lies in discovering new formulas or deciphering an old one. It's like Gianna's writing," he said as he cut his eye in her direction. "There are only twenty-six letters in the alphabet, but look at what she's been able to accomplish with just twenty-six letters!"

"Don't let my daughters fool you, Donovan. They may have hated their courses, but that was only because they were bored! Too smart for their own good, both of them!"

Franco pointed to Gianna. "This one, she has two advanced degrees in science and mathematics. She also speaks five languages. Brilliant, my girls are! Like their mother. My Angela, she was a genius, too!" he exclaimed. There was no missing the pride that filled the man's spirit.

Donovan tossed Gianna a look. "Five languages? You never told me that."

She laughed. "*Papà* is the only one who brags about me being a child prodigy!"

"I was no slacker now!" Carina said, moving them all to laugh again.

"Me," Franco concluded, "I'm glad I make wine. What you all do hurts my head!"

The laughter continued to be abundant, filling the room.

Donovan took a sip of the robust Cabernet in his

glass. The wine had been picked especially for the meal, a delightful complement to the dumpling-like pasta that had been filled with butternut squash, sage and goat cheese, served in a hazelnut brown-butter sauce with thick slices of freshly baked bread. "It's very good wine, by the way!"

Franco lifted his own glass in salute. "To new friends," he chanted as everyone joined him.

"New friends!"

"Donovan, would you like a tour of the winery?" Gianna asked as she pushed her chair from the table.

"I'd like that," he said with a nod of his head. He reached to clear his plate off the table.

"Don't you do that," Carina said, fanning her hands in his direction. "Graham and I will take care of the dishes."

"I'm always on dish duty," Graham said teasingly.

His wife leaned in to kiss his mouth. "Do good, honey, and I'll give you a treat later!"

Franco shook his head at the couple. "I think I'll take a walk through the gardens and enjoy a cigar. Donovan, I hope to see you again."

Donovan shook the man's outstretched hand. "Thank you again, sir," he said.

Gianna crooked her index finger and gestured for him to follow. Not needing a second invitation, Donovan went willingly.

For almost an hour, Gianna was the consummate professional as she gave him a guided tour of the grounds and winery. It was easy to see how passionate she was about her family's business and her role in its operations. Donovan was duly impressed.

The winery was substantial in size, and minutes into the tour he realized he knew very little about wine or its history. He was transfixed as Gianna schooled him.

"Many have called the Maremma the 'Wild West,' because of its landscapes and its wine-making. The Etruscans started making wine thousands of years before us in Northern Tuscany. They introduced viticulture to the Maremma in the nineteenth century."

"What is viticulture?" Donovan asked.

"Viticulture is the study of grapes and wine-making." Donovan nodded as she continued.

"The wines here in Maremma didn't become popular until the 1980s, and credit for putting us on the map goes to Marquis Mario Incisa della Rocchetta. Because of his efforts, we've created Bordeaux-style wines that are considered noble and refined. My father idolized him."

"Is he still in this area?"

"Sadly, he passed away in the 1980s. His son runs his winery now."

They moved to another area of the winery, stepping into a massive room that housed huge wooden barrels of wine that were resting to age. Gianna continued, explaining the process and even including a geography lesson.

"The Maremma is very different from other areas of Italy. Regions in the north, like northern Tuscany, Florence, Siena and Lucca, are always overrun with tourists. Their wineries cater to the tourism, and most of their cellars are always open to the general public. Not so much here. We are more exclusive, and the area is less populated with tourists.

"Serious wine lovers find us to be a very attractive region to visit. There's the town of Castiglione della Pescaia with its charming fishing port and castle, and Pitigliano, an amazing village completely carved out of the rocky outcrop below an ancient Jewish village. And one of my favorite places is Massa Marittima with its quaint cobblestoned streets. They're all fabulous little gems that you must explore while you're here in Tuscany."

Donovan stood in reflection, taking it all in. His arms were crossed over his chest, and he seemed as though he were lost deep in thought. Gianna found herself unable to take her eyes off him. His chiseled features were perfection, and she was suddenly imagining what it might be like to trace his profile with her finger. She stood in pause until he seemed ready to move on, tossing her a quick look and that dimpled smile.

"So, when do you find time to write?" he asked as the private tour came to a close.

Gianna chuckled warmly as they moved back outside, dropping to a wooden bench that decorated the gardens. She twisted her body around to face him.

"At night mostly, when I'm alone."

Donovan nodded as the two shared a gaze. They held it for a brief moment, the intensity almost combustible. As quickly as they connected, they both looked away. An awkward silence filled the space between them. He looked past her shoulder, staring off into the distance. Her eyes were cast down to the ground, and the blades of grass flattened beneath her leather sandals. They both cut their eyes back at each other at the same time. Then laughed to ease the tension.

"I didn't expect to be so nervous around you," Donovan said. "I feel like I'm fifteen all over again."

Gianna laughed. "I know, right!" She smiled. "I figured since we knew so much about each other that this would be easy."

He nodded, smiling back. He stared at her, taking in her delicate features as if casting each pore to memory. "You are so beautiful!" he exclaimed softly.

She laughed again, the gentle timbre a soft flutter that left him thinking of champagne bubbles and the gentle trickle of a waterfall.

"You're very sweet, Donovan Boudreaux."

He shifted forward in his seat. "Can I see you again tomorrow?"

"Don't you have classes tomorrow?"

"I have a commitment at the school in the morning, but I won't actually start teaching for another week. I'm free after the lunch hour tomorrow. And I really want to see you again!"

She grinned. "I know we have an inspection tomorrow, but once that's done I'll be free. Why don't you call me when you're done and we can make plans then?"

"Great!" Donovan exclaimed.

There was a pause before he finally stood. "I should be going. I don't want to overstay my welcome, and I'm sure you have things you need to get back to."

She shrugged. "You don't have to rush off on my account."

His full lips lifted up into a deep smile. "I wish I could stay, but I need to unpack and get settled in. Plus, I don't get the impression that Signora Rossi is going to tolerate me coming and going at all hours of the night." He extended his hand to help her up.

The touch was electric as her fingers gently glided against his. Both felt it, pulling away as if they'd been burned. Gianna's eyes were wide, and she inhaled swiftly. Donovan was suddenly aware of heat raging in his southern parts. He broke out into a cold sweat, perspiration beading against his brow.

"I'm glad you came to Tuscany, Donovan," Gianna said, her voice a soft whisper.

He nodded. "Me, too!"

The questions and comments came before Gianna could get the door closed behind Donovan's exit.

"Do you like him?"

"I think he was nice!"

"Why didn't you tell him the truth?"

"You really need to tell him the truth!"

"Are you going to see him again?"

"You really should see him again!"

Gianna laughed heartily as her family assaulted her with commentary. She held up her hand, amusement shimmering in her eyes.

"Donovan asked me to extend his gratitude to you all for a lovely evening. He said to tell you that he had a very nice time."

"Did you have a nice time, Sissy?" Carina leaned across the kitchen island, meeting her sister's stare.

Gianna shrugged slightly, her shoulders pushing toward the ceiling. "It was okay."

"Just okay?" Graham asked.

Franco laughed. "It was better than okay. Look at that grin on her face."

Gianna felt herself blush, color warming her cheeks a brilliant shade of crimson. She moved toward the door, tossing them all a slight wave of her hand, their laughter echoing behind her as she headed to her room.

Inside, with the door closed and locked, Gianna fell back against the bed, staring up toward the ceiling. Joy painted her expression. It had been a great day, and she'd had an exceptional time with Donovan Boudreaux. He hadn't been at all what she'd expected. Even after committing every word he'd written to her to memory, thinking that she had some sense of who the man was, she'd actually been surprised.

Donovan was a refreshing breath of air. His intelligence was complemented by a compassionate spirit and wicked sense of humor. And he didn't take himself seriously. She liked that he could laugh at himself, all the while bringing a smile to everyone else's face. His exuberance as they'd walked through the winery was almost childlike, and his enthusiasm had fueled her own. Donovan was multilayered, and she had only begun to scratch the surface to discover everything she could about him. Throw in his dashing good looks, and there was much to like about the math professor from the United States.

The decision to not tell him about Carina's little prank had come at the last minute. The moment she'd laid eyes on him, Gianna knew she didn't want to mar their first encounter with bad news. She could come clean in due time, she thought with a sigh. For now, all she wanted was to enjoy the magic that had her feeling giddy with happiness.

He was so excited by the afternoon's events that Donovan hadn't given any thought to how he planned to get back to his cottage. Luckily for him, the walk down the hillside was manageable. The sky was just beginning to darken. The cool evening air was comfortably warm with the gentlest of breezes pushing him forward. And as he headed downhill, he had a beautiful view of the Tuscan coast, the sun beginning to set over the bright blue water.

As he sauntered back to the village, he passed a spattering of homes that dotted the landscape. The area of Maremma was a host of everything that was extraordinary about Tuscany. There was blue sea, long beaches, black rock, hills covered with woods, marshes and flatlands, green hills, natural thermal baths and, most exquisite of them all, Gianna Martelli.

He felt lovestruck as he thought about the delightful woman who'd been everything he imagined and more. Beautiful didn't begin to describe her, inside or out. She had the purest spirit of any woman he'd ever known. There was something both delightful and decadent about her. Just the nearness of her had him giggling like an adolescent, and he couldn't remember any woman ever making him feel so frivolous.

To say that he was enamored with Gianna was putting it mildly. The woman left him breathless, and in that moment he was hard and wanting as thoughts of their time together frolicked through his memory. Gianna made his heart sing, and he was excited to see where their time together might take them.

As he passed a home that sat close to the roadside, there was a couple standing outside in deep conversation. Both looked up and eyed him warily as he moved in their direction. Donovan accepted that most in the community weren't used to seeing a large black man in their midst when it wasn't tourist season, and maybe not even then. He also imagined that seeing a large black man practically skipping with joy was a sight to behold, as well.

He raised a hand and waved excitedly, his bright smile warm and endearing. The husband gestured back with a nod of his head, the two suddenly talking rapidly in Italian. *"Buonasera!"* Donovan exclaimed as he got closer to the front gate of their property.

The wife greeted him cheerily, gesturing with both hands for him to come closer. As she spoke, he comprehended one, two, maybe three words of what she was saying, welcoming him to their village. Pausing in front of her, he was surprised when she reached up to grab his cheeks in her hands, squeezing his face as if he were six years old. His eyes widened with surprise as she pulled him close, kissing one side of his face and then the other.

Seconds later, her husband, who'd gone into the home, had come back through the door, a plate wrapped in a kitchen towel perched in the palms of his hands.

"Welcome!" the husband said as he extended the gift toward Donovan.

Donovan nodded. "Thank you!"

"You are the teacher, no?" the man questioned.

He bobbed his head a second time. "Yes, sir, I am."

"From my wife," the man gestured. "To say hello and welcome."

His wife said something in Italian, clearly passing on instructions to her spouse. He nodded and waved his hand for her to let him speak.

"My name is Fabrizio D'Ascenzi, and this is my wife, Pia."

"It's a pleasure to meet you, Signor D'Ascenzi! Signora D'Ascenzi, *ciao, mi chiamo* Donovan Boudreaux."

Signora D'Ascenzi grabbed his cheeks a second time. *"Piacere di conoscerti."*

Donovan nodded. "It's a pleasure to meet you, too, ma'am!"

"Pia has made her famous ricotta cheesecake to welcome you. It's the best cheesecake you will ever eat! All the women in the village have heard that you were coming to town, so I imagine you will eat well while you are here. All of them trying to marry off their daughters!"

Donovan laughed. "Do you and Signora D'Ascenzi have a daughter?"

The man shook his head. "No. If we did, you wouldn't be getting this cheesecake," he said with a hearty chuckle. "I would have had her make you a five-course meal!"

His wife punched him playfully, and Donovan realized that she understood English better than she spoke it.

"Well, thank you," Donovan said.

"Where are you headed?" Signor D'Ascenzi asked, looking up the road one way and then the other.

As Donovan explained his predicament, the couple nodded in understanding.

"Now, those are two beautiful women!" the other man exclaimed. "Franco's daughters are very easy on a man's eyes! But only one is unmarried, no?"

He nodded. "Yes, sir."

He said something to his wife in Italian that Donovan didn't understand. She responded with a wave of her head, her hands tossed in the air in frustration.

Donovan looked at one and then another, suddenly feeling like the ball in a tennis match.

Signor D'Ascenzi flipped his hand at the woman as she suddenly turned, muttering under her breath as she stomped into her home.

Donovan looked on, confused, as her husband gestured for him to follow him to his truck, offering him a ride for the rest of his journey. Once they were headed down the road, his new acquaintance explained the conversation.

"My wife says you need to watch that Martelli girl. That one is too wild for such a distinguished professor as yourself. And she has a tongue like a viper! You might want to walk to the vineyards on the other side and introduce yourself to the Carusos' daughter. She's round like a barrel and has the face of an old cow, but she's quite the cook and she doesn't talk a lot."

Donovan laughed heartily. As Signor D'Ascenzi continued, his assessments of the women in the community sometimes moving him to tears, he knew beyond any doubt that moving to Italy had been the best decision he could have ever made.

Chapter 5

The following morning Donovan rose bright and early. Signora Rossi was knocking on the door minutes after he'd stepped out of the shower, chattering a mile a minute. She'd pushed her way inside, armed with a plate of warm baked pastries, a pot of hot coffee and a basket of fresh fruit.

The conversation was very one-sided, although she chatted as if they were old friends. Every so often she would pause to look at him as if she expected an answer to something she'd said. A simple nod of his head and a smile with an occasional yes sent her back to talking without skipping a beat. Donovan found himself hoping that by the end of the year, he'd understand enough to hold a full conversation in Italian, or at least enough to know if he were promising the old woman his first-born child.

After his stomach was full and his head clear, he watched as his new house mother commenced cleaning and sweeping behind him. With a wave of his hand, he wished her a good day and headed outside to meet the groundskeeper. His new friend handed him an old road map, a functioning GPS and the keys to an older model Fiat 500 parked in the driveway, a perk to his residency.

The drive to Siena and the university had been breathtaking. Donovan was quickly discovering that he loved everything about Italy. He was eager to play tourist and visit Rome. To see the Colosseum and the ruins, the Spanish Steps, the Vatican and the Sistine Chapel. Florence was also on his must-see list, and he wanted to lose himself in the stunning architecture.

As the GPS barked out a turn, guiding him closer to his destination, he suddenly found himself hopeful that Gianna might want to share in those experiences with him.

For a few brief moments Donovan stood outside the university, taking it all in. The building was massive, the old-world architecture like nothing he'd seen before. The magnitude of all his accomplishments that had brought him to this place suddenly rang through to his core as he understood the significance of the blessing that had been bestowed on him. He whispered a quick prayer, snapped a photo with his cell phone and texted a message to his mother.

Sophie was standing at the campus entrance, waiting to greet him. The head of the mathematics department, she was tall and lean like a racehorse with skin the color of dark mahogany. Her hair was shaved close, accentuating her chiseled features. She reminded him of the model Alek Wek, her exotic look distinct to her African lineage. She was an attractive woman who carried herself with refined grace. Her pleasant personality was endearing, and since their very first meeting, she'd been eager to learn from him and he'd found that flattering. More than anything, he considered her a friend and looked forward to the opportunity to work with her.

Sophie welcomed him warmly, eagerly wrapping him in a tight hug. She grabbed both his hands between her own. "*Buongiorno!* This is so exciting!" she exclaimed.

"Good morning, Sophie! How are you this morning?"

"I'm fantastic. How about yourself? Did you settle in comfortably?"

"I did. Everything is perfect."

"That's so good to hear. I was concerned. When you requested to be housed in Maremma, I had my doubts. Plus, I worried that the commute might be problematic."

"Actually, the drive was delightful. I'm about an hour away, but it will give me a chance to prepare myself in the mornings and unwind in the evenings. But I like Maremma. It's quiet where I am, and I like being away from the hustle and bustle of city life."

She nodded. "Well, let me get you settled in and show you to your office."

Leading the way, Sophie began by introducing him

to the school's director, Dr. Alistair Northway. He was a small man who spoke English as if he were spitting bullets after each word. At first glance, he reminded Donovan of a white Kevin Hart with flaming red hair and a toothy grin. As they shook hands, Donovan noticed that the man's grip was Herculean. He felt as though he were trying to break his fingers. But his words were kind as he welcomed Donovan to his staff, lauding his many accomplishments and acknowledging the faith he had in what they'd all be able to accomplish for the good of his students.

In the school's administrative offices, he'd been assigned a parking space, taken a photo for his identification badge and filled out more employment papers than he cared to count. After an hour, the names and faces had become a blur. He met most of the department chairs, a number of instructors and probably twice as many students.

Finally, he stood at the head of his lecture room, taking it all in. The space felt more like an old movie theater auditorium with upholstered velvet seats and antique finishes. His oversize desk and the chalkboard on the front wall kept the reality of the moment intact. As he leaned back against his desk, Donovan fought back hot tears that burned behind his eyelids. Loving to teach as much as he did made the experience all the sweeter. It was going to be a very good year.

Gianna's cell phone rang just as she was packing an assortment of items into a large wicker basket. She answered on the third ring, propping the device between her ear and shoulder. *"Ciao!"*

"Gianna, hello! It's Donovan."

"Donovan, hello," she answered, her tone rising. "How are you?"

"I'm really good, but I'll be even better if you say you can still spend some time with me this afternoon."

She laughed. "I think that can be arranged. What did you have in mind?"

"I wasn't sure, to be honest with you. I thought maybe we could grab something to eat and you could give me a tour of the city?"

There was a pause as Gianna seemed to be reflecting on his proposition. "Are you still at the university?" she asked suddenly.

"Yes. I should be leaving here in about an hour, then it's a good hour commute. I'll just need to stop home and change."

"Good. I'll meet you when you get there," she said. Then before he could respond, she disconnected the call, leaving Donovan hanging on the other end.

Carina laughed. "So, are you playing hard to get with Donovan, or easy breezy?"

Gianna tossed her sister a look. "I'm not playing anything with the man. Not yet anyway!"

Carina giggled again. "Oh, you're up to something. I don't know what it is, but I know you."

Gianna grinned. "Maybe I am, and maybe I'm not. We'll just have to see."

"Poor Donovan," Carina said, shaking her head. "He doesn't have a clue what's about to hit him!"

Gianna laughed with her sister, not bothering to respond to the comment. "I have someplace to be," she said as she grabbed the handles of her picnic basket and headed toward the door.

Carina waved goodbye. "Tell Donovan I said hello!"

As Donovan moved to the door of his new home, his landlady poked her head out of her own entrance. Her gaze was narrowed, her jaw tight as she gnashed her teeth together. He instinctively knew she wasn't happy about something.

"*Ciao!* Signora Rossi!" He raised a hand in greeting.

He was suddenly reminded of a bird cackling nonstop as she berated him about something, her index finger wagging as frantically as her tongue. Before he could think to respond, his own door flew open and Gianna stepped outside. Both women were suddenly in heated conversation, hands waving excitedly to make a point.

Gianna suddenly said something that gave Signora Rossi reason to pause. The older woman stood staring for just a brief moment, and then she burst out laughing. When Gianna laughed with her, Donovan sighed with relief, thankful that whatever had been amiss between the two women hadn't brought them to blows.

He looked from one to the other as their conversation continued, tones lowered and amusement dancing in their words. "Do I even want to know?" Donovan asked after Signora Rossi waved her finger at him one last time before going back into her home, leaving the two of them alone.

Gianna smiled. "She's worried about your virtue. Afraid that I may take advantage and sully your upstanding reputation."

He laughed with her. "Is there something about *you* I need to know?" he asked.

She laughed with him. "I guess that depends on who you ask!"

"Should I be scared?"

Ignoring his question, Gianna turned an about-face and moved back into his home.

Donovan followed behind her. As he moved through the door he came to an abrupt halt, his eyes skating back and forth over the space inside. "When did you…? How did this…?" he stammered, fighting to focus and find the words to ask the thoughts suddenly racing through his head.

When he'd left that morning, the sun had been on the other side of the small unit, yet to stream brightly through his windows. Signora Rossi had been sweeping the tile floors with one hand and dusting the wood furniture with the other. His suitcases had rested on the pullout sofa in the room, waiting to be unpacked. And the whole space lacked the personal touches that would eventually make it feel like a home.

But since he'd been gone, the entire room had been transformed. The windows were all open, a warm breeze billowing through the space. Light was abundant, bright and sweeping from one wall to the other. Fresh flowers had been strategically placed, and a potted cactus rested on the kitchen counter. There was a tablecloth on the kitchen table and appliances on the counter in the small kitchenette. Beautifully woven throws decorated the sofa and chairs, with complementary pillows adorning the corners. And the framed photos that had been in his luggage were placed strategically around the room, with the photo of him and his parents sitting front and center on a bookcase.

"Wow!" he exclaimed as he moved farther into the room. "Wow!" He tossed her a quick look as he spun around in a circle, taking it all in.

"All your clothes are unpacked, and there are extra linens in the closet. I know you like to eat clean so there's a blender *and* a juicer, and the icebox is fully stocked with fresh fruit and vegetables. I told Signora Rossi that she needs to replace the lightbulbs in the bathroom. They really do need to be brighter, and she said she'd have someone take care of it while we're gone." Gianna paused to take a breath. "Now, I hope you haven't had anything to eat because I packed us a picnic lunch."

Donovan rested his gaze on her face. She wore no makeup, her warm complexion crystal clear, her hair pulled back into a loose bun. She was glowing, looking like a freshly minted penny. She stood in denim shorts and a Bob Marley T-shirt, and if Donovan were a betting man, he would have bet his last dollar that she wasn't wearing a bra, her breasts at full attention beneath her top. He struggled not to stare at her chest.

Gianna broke the trance he'd fallen into. "You should change. Something casual. I left your jeans and a black T-shirt on the bed for you."

He smiled. "Are you always so…?"

"Controlling?"

"Efficient."

She smiled back. "Efficient…no. Controlling…yes!"

He nodded, still eyeing her as she pointed him in the direction of his bedroom.

Stepping into the room, he closed the door behind him. The bedding was new, an assortment of pillows leaning against the wicker headboard. A stack of books rested on the nightstand. The titles made him smile. There was an advanced reading copy of Gianna's next book, a Fodor's travel guide for Italy, a children's book by Shel Silverstein and an official King James Bible. But the single greatest surprise was the framed photograph of Gianna, an image of her standing between rows of olive trees. She wore a white dress that complemented her warm complexion, and her smile was sweet, a hint of mischief dancing in her eyes.

As Donovan rested the frame back on the nightstand, he couldn't help but think that Gianna had officially laid claim to her territory. A huge grin filled his dark face—he was happy to have been claimed. He was overwhelmed with everything she'd done, amazed by the effort she'd put forth on his behalf. No woman had ever done anything like that for him before. Ever.

Minutes later the two were headed inland to Mount Amiata, the largest of the lava domes in the area. Their conversation was easy, a comfortable exchange that felt like they'd been conversing forever. Donovan told her about his day and his excitement over his teaching job. She explained the inspection process that allowed the winery to remain operational and how the periodic scrutiny always gave her anxiety. They talked about books, hers, topping bestseller lists worldwide, and his, the mathematical publications preeminent only in educational circles. And they laughed, abundantly, the richness of it like the sweetest balm in the afternoon air.

He asked questions about where they were and where they were going, and Gianna infused the geography lesson with history and anecdotes. She described the area as one of the regions most unmarred by its inhabitants. The beaches were pristine, the umbrella-shaped maritime pines unique and the cork-oak woodlands abundant. As they passed another wine estate near Orbetello, he was in awe of the spotted pink flamingos that grazed in a lagoon.

In Amiata they moved from the car to the trails, hiking through the luxuriant trees. Donovan was dazzled by the wealth of color that decorated the landscape. He suddenly wished he could paint, that he was able to capture the striking images in an organic manner. Speaking his wish aloud had Gianna encouraging him to step out of his comfort zone to try things he'd never tried before.

"If that's what you want to do, then you should, Donovan," she said. "People are always waiting until the perfect time, or the right moment to do things. But life is too short to put off things you want to do. No one's promised you tomorrow."

He nodded his agreement, although his expression seemed to say that he was still mulling it over.

"So do you plan to start painting while you are here in Italy?" she asked as they continued to navigate the trails.

He shrugged, his eyes wide as he stared at her. "I'll do it," he said, a wry smile pulling at his lips. "Soon."

She laughed at him. "You are too funny!"

"You know I have to analyze everything, Gianna. Weigh all the pros and cons. I need to be certain before I commit to something."

"Or miss out on opportunities because you take too long doing all that thinking!"

Donovan chuckled softly. "I really am not that bad."

"Maybe not, but you need to be more spontaneous. You and I will work on that while you are here."

He smiled as she turned off the path and headed through the trees. He trailed behind her, following where she led. Minutes later Gianna found a perfect spot for them to picnic, and set to work covering the ground with an oversize blanket. She gestured for him to take a seat, and when he did she pulled off his shoes and socks and tossed them aside. As he wiggled his toes, he watched as she stood and kicked off her own shoes before taking a seat beside him.

Inside the picnic basket she'd made him carry, she had packed a light afternoon meal. There was an assortment of cheeses, salami, olives, two loaves of fresh bread, an assortment of fresh fruit, a bottle of her father's wine and two wine goblets.

"Do you come here often?" he asked as he took a bite of a creamy Asiago cheese.

"Not nearly as often as I'd like," she answered. "I love this area, though. Next to my father's vineyards, it's one of my favorite places." She tore off a bite of bread and popped it into her mouth.

A blanket of quiet dropped around them as they sat focused on the meal. Neither spoke, both seeming to drop into their own thoughts. In the distance a voice called out, someone besieging a friend not to hurry so fast. Between the trees, they caught a glimpse of denim-covered legs and a small dog on the end of a leash. They both paused to stare at the same time, watching the small terrier race to get to someone ahead of them.

Donovan shifted his gaze to her face, noting the color that had risen to her cheeks. She smiled, and he felt his stomach do a slight flip. He cleared his throat, suddenly feeling nervous for no reason at all.

"What?" Gianna asked suddenly.

"What do you mean what?"

"What are you staring at me like that for?"

"I wasn't staring at you."

"Yes, you were!"

"Well, if I was it's only because you're so beautiful."

Gianna rolled her eyes. She reached for a grape and pulled it to her mouth, not bothering to respond.

Donovan cleared his throat. "I wrote once and asked if you were in a relationship, and you didn't respond. Was there a reason?"

She met the look he was giving her, curiosity furrowing his brow. She shook her head. "I'm sure I answered."

"No, you didn't."

"I'm sure I did."

He pursed his lips, then pulled them into a deep smile. "Stop ignoring the question, Gianna. Are you seeing someone?"

She laughed. "I wasn't ignoring the question! But to give you an answer, no, I'm not. Are you?"

He hesitated for a brief second. "Well…actually…" His gaze skated off into the distance.

Gianna bristled ever so slightly, sitting straighter as she folded her extended legs behind her. She shifted forward as if readying herself to stand and leave. "Actually what? You wrote that you weren't dating anyone," she said, an air of attitude in her tone. "I distinctly remember reading that. So was that a lie?"

A wide grin spread full across Donovan's face. "Gotcha!"

She narrowed her gaze, not at all amused.

"I was joking!" Donovan exclaimed. "You told me I needed to loosen up and stop taking things so seriously. So why are you mad?"

She shook her head. "I'm not mad. I just didn't find your little joke funny."

He laughed heartily. "Gianna Martelli has a little bit of a jealous streak," he teased.

"I do not!"

"Yes, you do." He reached for her hand, entwining her fingers between his own. His touch was electric, the current between them combustible. "And I kind of like it," he said, his voice dropping to a loud whisper. "But if I'm honest," he continued after another brief pause, "I'm really hoping that you and I are seeing each other. Or getting close to that point."

The hint of a smile danced across her face. His touch was heated, fire coursing through her palm, up the length of her arm and exploding with a vengeance through her body. A shiver ran down her spine and back up, the sensations close to orgasmic.

She suddenly pulled her hand from his, color heating her cheeks. Turning her body around, she lay back against him, resting her head in his lap. She pulled a grape from the bunch in her hands and slid it into her mouth.

Donovan felt the muscles in his lower half twitch as he watched her chew, her mouth rolling in the cutest pout. Just the hint of tongue peeked past the line of her of her lips, the gesture teasing. He closed his eyes and inhaled swiftly, fighting to stall the rise of nature.

Gianna shifted his attention away from his growing predicament by changing the subject. "Why aren't you married, Donovan? You're successful, handsome and intelligent. For all intents and purposes, most would consider you a good catch, so why hasn't some equally accomplished, beautiful and smart woman gotten you to the altar?"

Donovan pondered her question for a moment. Over the years his personal life had taken a backseat to his professional one. Even as his siblings were building relationships, finding favor with significant others, he'd been focused on his career. At best, dating had been hit or miss, no woman ever catching his full attention. Until he'd started corresponding with Gianna.

His gaze met hers as she stared up at him, still waiting for him to answer. Curiosity seeped from her stare, questions shimmering in the light that shone in the dark orbs, and he could feel himself falling headfirst into the depths of her gaze.

He finally answered. "I was waiting for you," he said softly, the early evening air carrying his words away on a warm breeze.

Chapter 6

Gianna felt giddy. Lovesick giddy, and she hated not being able to hide it. But the emotion flooded her face. It seeped from every pore in her body. And it wasn't going away. It had taken every ounce of fortitude not to giggle like a little girl when Donovan had said that he'd been waiting for her. Instead, she'd changed the subject again, rambling on and on about the merits of olives and wine for one's health.

She blew a soft sigh as she rolled onto her side, a good night's sleep promising to elude her. They'd spent the entire afternoon together, moving from the forests of Amiata to La Guardiola, a local bar in the area that she often frequented. The Rossella Graziani Jazz Trio had been performing, and the atmosphere had been seductive. The staff there knew her by name, and her favorite drink was delivered to their table before either had a chance to get comfortable in their seats.

There wasn't much that they hadn't talked about, although Gianna had purposely avoided any conversation that might have led them back to what was happening between them. Donovan had tried more than once to steer their talk to things more personal, but she had shut him down, not yet ready to voice what she found herself feeling. Because Gianna wasn't ready to label their relationship. It was too new to her, and even though she understood he had more time and energy invested in their connection, she was still gun-shy where Donovan Boudreaux was concerned.

But she did like him. She liked him a lot. Even his conservative nature, which was so contrary to her own, thrilled her. They balanced each other nicely, and most surprising to her was how comfortable she felt when she was with him. That level of comfort had been apparent from day one. There had only been a few moments of anxiety, and that apprehension had everything to do with her attraction to the man and the rising desire that seemed to consume her every time he was near.

Because every time Donovan was close, Gianna found herself heated with desire. The intensity of her longing was almost like an out-of-body experience. Gianna had never wanted any man like she found herself wanting Donovan, and her body reacted on its own accord each and every time.

With a deep sigh, she rolled to the other side of the bed, curling her body around an oversize pillow. An

hour later she drifted off to sleep, thoughts of Donovan
still trailing through her mind.

Donovan sat upright in the full-size bed, Gianna's
upcoming book in his lap. It was everything he imagined it would be and more. The woman's talent and
imagination awed him as he wondered where she found
the inspiration that breathed life into her mysteries.
Clearly she loved what she did, but Donovan knew that
she was ambivalent about her achievements, wanting
only to enjoy the peace and quiet of her Tuscany home.
Her writing was an added perk to her resort-like lifestyle, but she would have easily given it up to work the
vineyards.

Admittedly, he was starstruck, idolizing everything
about her. Donovan imagined that he probably came
across a tad fan-crazed, and he couldn't help but wonder
if his enthusiasm might be perceived as a little creepy.
He blew a heavy sigh as he closed the cover of her book.
He shifted his body against the headboard and heaved
another deep sigh.

He had wanted them to talk more about the two of
them and their growing relationship, but Gianna had
changed the subject each and every time. It felt as if he
might be reading more into the connection he thought
they had than she did. And maybe she wasn't feeling
him the way he was feeling her. Because he was feeling
her, feeling bewitched and spellbound by all things Gianna. But he had more concerns and questions than he
had answers. He suddenly wondered if he should have

been more open about his growing emotions before coming to Italy and potentially getting his feelings hurt.

Rising, he crossed the room to shut off the lights, then crawled back into the bed. He stole a glance at the alarm clock on the nightstand, the early morning hour shining back at him. Sleep had not been his friend; he was unable to turn off the thoughts running through his mind. He missed Gianna. The day had been exceptional. They'd had a great time together, and it had ended earlier than he would have liked. Now he was missing the woman who had him tossing and turning, unable to get her out of his head.

The ringing telephone pulled Donovan from a deep sleep. Startled, he jumped, then struggled to find his cell phone. He'd practically fallen out of the bed when he finally pulled it to his ear, shouting "hello" into the receiver.

Kendrick laughed on the other end. "Hey, big brother. What's going on?"

Donovan sat upright in the bed, blinking his eyes rapidly as he struggled to focus. The faintest hint of light shimmered through the sheer curtain that covered the one window in the space.

"Kendrick?"

"Yeah! Are you okay?"

"Nothing that another couple of hours of sleep won't fix."

"You're sleeping late? That's not like you at all."

Donovan yawned. "I didn't get a lot of sleep."

"Oh. Are you not alone? Because I can call back if you have company."

Donovan could sense his brother grinning into the phone. He shook his head. "No, I don't have company."

"You and your friend haven't hooked up yet?"

"We've spent time together." Donovan could feel himself blushing, heat warming his cheeks. "But not like that."

"But you've hung out! That's good, right? So, what's she like?"

There was a pause as Donovan found himself once again lost in thoughts of Gianna. "I like her," he said finally. "And I think Mom is really going to like her, too."

This time Kendrick paused for a quick moment before responding. "Is it that serious? I thought you were just looking to hit it and quit it, sort of like a holiday fling. But you're thinking you want to introduce her to the old people?"

"Yes," Donovan said softly. "I think Gianna's the kind of girl you definitely take home to meet your family. She's special."

"And she feels the same way about you?"

He shrugged, doubt suddenly flooding his spirit. When he didn't respond, Kendrick turned the conversation, sensing Donovan wasn't prepared yet to answer questions about his new friend and her feelings.

"I had some time before I head back to the States, so I thought I might swing by and check out your place so I can give the girls the four-one-one. They've already called me a half-dozen times to see what I know, and I might have mentioned something about you and Gianna. I figured a few cell-phone photos would get them off both our backs."

Donovan laughed. "*Might* have mentioned?"

"Yeah, it might have slipped out during a conversation or two, but that's neither here nor there. You know how nosy the girls are. We have to give them something or they might show up on your doorstep to see for themselves."

Donovan shook his head. "Those are your sisters!"

"They were your sisters before they were mine," Kendrick said, laughing with him.

Donovan suddenly realized how much he missed his family. "What time can you be here?"

When the Martelli twins pulled up in front of Donovan's cottage, he and his brother were standing outside in conversation. The two sisters shot each other a look, a wry smile pulling at Carina's thin lips. "Oh, my!" she muttered, her voice dropping to a low whisper.

"Don't you dare embarrass me," Gianna hissed under her breath.

Carina giggled softly.

"I mean it," Gianna countered, cutting an eye at her sister.

Carina giggled again, meeting the look her twin was giving her. "What?"

Gianna looked from one man to the other, immediately noting the resemblance. No one needed to tell her that they were somehow related. Like Donovan, the other man was a dark, tall drink of water. He wore his hair in a full afro, and he was dressed in low-slung, tattered jeans, a T-shirt adorned with a Duke University emblem and rugged Timberland boots. But his demeanor seemed more bad boy and deviant, not nearly as conservative as Donovan's. Side by side, the two men were like night and day, yet everything about them was similar.

As the two women approached, Donovan's smile pulled full and bright across his face. He tossed up an easy hand and gave the two women a slight wave. "Hello!" he greeted cheerily.

"Hi," Carina said, almost too enthusiastically.

Gianna shot her sister another look, grabbing her forearm in warning. She nodded in greeting. "How are you?"

Donovan gestured toward them. "Let me introduce you to my brother. Kendrick, this is Gianna Martelli and her sister, Carina Martelli-Porter. These two ladies run the winery up the hill along with their father and Carina's husband. Ladies, this is my brother, Kendrick Boudreaux."

"It's nice to meet you," Carina said as she extended a hand.

"Kendrick, hello!" Gianna greeted.

"The pleasure is all mine," Kendrick replied, a bright smile pulling at his full lips. "It's nice to meet you both."

"You didn't tell us your brother was coming to visit," Gianna said as she eased her way to Donovan's side. The two exchanged a look, their stare intense. The connection was intoxicating, and it was only when Carina faked a cough that they turned back to the conversation, self-consciously giggling.

Kendrick responded to the young woman's remark. "I'm just passing through. I finished some business in Florence earlier than anticipated and figured I'd make a quick stop here to check on Donovan before I made my way back to the States."

Donovan rolled his eyes. "So what are you two up to?" His gaze shifted back toward Gianna as his voice dropped an octave. "I didn't think I was going to see you today."

The two sisters traded a look, something secretive passing between them. Carina lifted her eyebrows, seeming to wait for Gianna to take the lead.

Gianna answered. "Carina and I were headed to the market and just wanted to see if you were interested in tagging along," she said, tossing her twin another strained look.

Kendrick tapped his brother on the back. "They want you to tag along to market, big brother! That sounds like fun! And I can take pictures!"

Neither woman missed the amusement in the man's tone as color flooded Donovan's face a deep shade of embarrassed. He shot his brother a look as the other man suddenly pulled out his cell phone and engaged the camera on the device. Before either could say cheese, he snapped the side-by-side shot of Donovan and Gianna standing just millimeters from each other.

Donovan shook his head. "It does sound like fun," he finally said. "We'd love to join you."

Hours later, joined by Graham, the five of them sat around a table at an outdoor bistro sipping on short shots of espresso from demitasse cups as they snacked on cannoli pastry shells filled with a mixture of chocolate chips and ricotta cheese and garnished with slivered almonds. Laughter rang through the air as they shared stories and anecdotes about each other.

"We never could get Donovan to jump with us," Kendrick was saying, a wide smile on his face. "All of us gave it a shot, but not him."

"I wasn't that crazy," Donovan said, amusement painting his expression. "It was all fun and games right up to when Kendrick missed the mattress and broke his arm."

Gianna laughed. "I can't imagine a bunch of little kids jumping out of a window onto a mattress."

Donovan nodded. "Well, my brothers and sisters did. The girls dared the boys so they all jumped two stories down."

"And I only missed the mattress because my twin, Kamaya, pushed me!"

They all laughed.

"Sounds like you all were a handful. And I thought our father had it hard with the two of us," Carina said as she exchanged a look with Gianna.

"Were you two a challenge?" Donovan asked, looking from one to the other.

Gianna nodded. "We weren't easy, I'll say that."

"Kamaya and I weren't too bad together," Kendrick said. "The best we could muster up was our secret language that none of the others understood. It used to drive our oldest sister crazy!"

Donovan nodded. "It never bothered us boys, but the girls hated it!"

Graham chuckled. "These two liked to play practical jokes pretending to be each other. Almost got me in serious trouble when we were in college and I was trying to get Carina's attention."

The twins laughed. Carina drew a warm palm across her husband's broad back as she wrapped herself around him. "We were only testing you, baby," she said.

Graham laughed. "Some test!"

Gianna smiled brightly at the two of them. She turned her attention toward Donovan's brother. "So, Kendrick, how long do you plan to be here? We'd love to invite you to the winery for dinner and the grand tour."

Kendrick nodded. "I appreciate that, but I have to fly out tonight. But if the invitation stands, I'd love to take you up on it the next time I'm in town. I hope to get back sometime soon and bring my wife. Vanessa and I have never seen Italy together."

"Since you two eloped, maybe you can have an official celebration here with the family?" Donovan suggested.

"We can do a fabulous reception at the winery!" Carina added. "Graham and I were actually married in the olive groves, and that's a beautiful option if you want to take your vows again."

Kendrick laughed as he held up his hands. "Slow it down! Y'all are moving way too fast. Let me talk it over with my favorite girl, and I'll get back to you. Vanessa's almost done with school, and then we'll take it from there."

"What is your wife studying?" Graham asked.

"She's a documentary film major."

"That's exciting!" Carina said.

Kendrick tossed a quick glance toward his wristwatch. "I hate to run because this has been a great time, but I need to get a taxi back to the airport."

"We can give you a ride," Graham said, looking toward his wife. "Carina and I need to head back, as well."

"Or you can ride with me and Donovan," Gianna said, looking around the table.

Donovan shook his head. "Gianna and I don't need to rush off," he said, his brow raised. "Thanks, Graham."

Kendrick laughed. "Yes, Graham, thank you. I appreciate the offer," the man replied as he stood up.

Gianna and her sister exchanged a look, a sly smile lifting Gianna's mouth.

Carina rose to her husband's side. "Well, I guess we will catch up with you two later," she said as she leaned down to kiss Donovan's cheek. "Don't let her scare you," she whispered into his ear.

He laughed as Kendrick shook his hand, tapped fists and bumped his shoulder. "I'll call you when I get home," he said.

His brother nodded. "Safe travels."

Goodbyes and well wishes rang out between them until Gianna's sister and brother-in-law and Donovan's brother had made their exit, the car pulling off in the direction of the airport.

A soft lull wafted between the couple as the two settled into the sudden quiet. Gianna reached for a cannoli that rested on Donovan's plate and took a large bite. As she chewed, she extended the decadent pastry in his direction, pausing as she reached his lips. Clasping his palm over her hand, he took his own bite of the dessert, his eyes locked on her face.

Her stare was teasing, heat flickering in the dark orbs. Their gazes danced in perfect synchronization, flitting back and forth in an easy give-and-take. Gianna was the first to break the silence.

"So why did you think we wouldn't see each other today?" she asked.

"Excuse me?"

"Earlier you said that you didn't think you were going to see me today. Why was that?" She slowly scooped a trail of chocolate from the plate with her finger, easing the decadent treat past her lips.

Donovan's eyes lifted as he shrugged. He cleared his throat before speaking. "I thought I might have been a little pushy yesterday. I was worried that you were put off by me trying to define our relationship."

Her head bobbed ever so slightly as she seemed to be reflecting on his comment. She leaned forward in her seat as she slowly licked the cream filling from her fingers. Eyeing her, Donovan felt a rush of heat course through his body, the seductive motion like a lit match igniting a low flame between them. He opened his mouth to speak, but nothing came out. The gesture was distracting, and he was suddenly at a loss for words, unable to form a coherent thought as he watched her suck her index finger slowly.

He closed his eyes and shook his head, then waved his own finger in her direction. "You're a tease!" he said, amusement dancing in his tone. "You're a tease, and you're enjoying every minute of this! You're also trying to distract me from having this conversation."

Gianna laughed as she wiped her hands on a paper napkin. "I don't know what you're talking about."

"You know exactly what I'm talking about and what you were doing." He shifted toward her, easing his body closer to hers. They were practically nose to nose as he held her gaze. "You're teasing me, and I fell for it."

There was a brief moment of silence before she nodded, her eyes wide as she eased back in her seat, needing to fill the space between them with a waft of cool air. Once again, Gianna changed the subject.

"So why do we need to define our relationship?"

Donovan sighed softly before answering. "We don't, but it would be nice to know where I stand with you." He shifted closer a second time, his leg pressing hot against hers. "Because I really care about you, Gianna. I know we just met, but what's happening between us has been building for months now. So why can't we just say it? Unless I'm reading something into our friendship that's not there?"

She shook her head, her eyes skating from side to side as she tried to think. A wave of anxiety suddenly flooded her spirit, washing over her sensibilities. She took a deep breath and then another before speaking. "Donovan, you already know where you and I stand. You and I are friends. Very *good* friends. What more do you need to know…or want me to say about us?"

Donovan sat back in his seat, still staring at her. That nervous twitch he'd noticed before was suddenly quiv-

ering, the muscle in her face dancing of its own volition. She suddenly drew her fingers to her face as if to
will it to stop. Gianna shifted her gaze from his, and he
could almost feel the wave of anxiety that had dropped
like a blanket around her shoulders. For the first time
Donovan sensed that Gianna wasn't as certain as she
wanted people to believe. The tough veneer she exuded
had cracked, exposing an air of fragility that he'd not
sensed before.

Gianna took a deep inhale of air and held it, silently
counting to ten before blowing it slowly past her parted
lips. Donovan's intense stare had her quivering with
nervous excitement. She was suddenly feeling vulnerable and transparent, as if he could see right through
her. He wanted to define them, to hear her say what was
clearly in his heart. But even in his certainty, she felt
most uncertain, something like fear clutching her heart.
And then he smiled, the beauty of it like the sweetest
balm, and all she could do was smile with him.

Donovan reached into his wallet, pulling money from
inside to leave a tip. He rested the ten euro banknote in
the center of the table. Standing, he extended his hand
toward her. As she slid her fingers between his, their
touch was electric…and comforting.

"We should go," he said softly, pulling her to her feet.

Gianna nodded, suddenly wishing she could find
the words to tell him that she really didn't want to. If
she were honest, she wasn't ready to tell him goodbye.

Chapter 7

Donovan stood at the window, looking out over the landscape. The ride back had been exceptionally quiet, neither he nor Gianna knowing what to say. For the first time since connecting with the woman, he felt as if she was a stranger, and he couldn't begin to understand why.

He turned back to the textbooks that lined his kitchen table. He needed to finalize his teaching plan for the first semester, but his mind wasn't on the curriculum. Donovan was feeling out of sorts about what had happened between him and Gianna. Or more accurately, what wasn't happening. He hadn't wanted to push, sensing that she would have felt as if she was being backed into a corner. And then it had dawned on him that what he had hoped for between them was probably not meant to be.

He sighed deeply as he moved back to the table and

took a seat. As he pored over the documents before him, he was desperate to focus his attention on anything that would take his mind off Gianna. But time seemed to drag as he tried to fix his mind on the numbers he so loved to manipulate.

The knock on his front door startled him. Donovan looked toward the clock on the wall. It was well after midnight, and he couldn't begin to imagine who'd be paying him a visit at such a late hour. The knock came a second time, the rapping abrupt and impatient. Moving from his seat to the door, he opened it just enough to peek out.

Gianna stood on the other side, eyeing him as warily as he eyed her. "I didn't think you'd be sleeping," she said matter-of-factly.

"Why not?"

"Because you're still thinking about the two of us."

He paused, wanting to tell her she was wrong. But he couldn't, as the words would prove to be a lie. Instead he shrugged his shoulders. "What are you doing here?"

"I came to talk…about us," she said as she pushed her way past him. As she turned to stare, she was taken aback, her breath catching deep in her chest. Her eyes grew big as her gaze ran the length of his body to the floor and back. Donovan was wearing a pair of cotton sleeping pants and little else. Bare-chested, he reminded her of a cover model for a men's magazine or a steamy romance novel. Clearly he took meticulous care of his body, his skin smooth like melted chocolate. He had the pecs of a body builder, and his abdominal muscles were easily a rippled eight-pack.

Before she could catch herself, Gianna reached out to trail her hand across his torso, gasping loudly as her fingertips connected with his flesh. Her eyes suddenly widened as she snatched her hand back, mortified that she'd been so brazen. Donovan took a step toward her.

"I should probably go put something on," he said, his voice a loud whisper.

"No… Yes… I mean…!" she sputtered, meeting his gaze. She clasped her hand to her chest as she turned and hurried back to the door. "I'll be waiting for you out here," she called over her shoulder.

Donovan shook his head, a smile blossoming across his face. Moving into his bedroom, he slipped his bare feet into a pair of leather sandals and pulled on a T-shirt, then he headed out the door after her.

Outside, Gianna still clutched her hand close to her chest, feeling as if it had been burned. Her fingers tingled, the quivers going all the way down to her toes. Just the briefest touch had her wanting to splay herself open to the man, to give him a taste of her sweets and treats. Donovan Boudreaux had her imagining the two of them in the most compromising positions, heated and dirty and pleasurable beyond measure.

She took a deep breath, gulping air as if her life depended on it. She suddenly found herself having a change of heart, not knowing if coming to see Donovan had been a good idea, after all. When she'd tiptoed out of the farmhouse, she'd known exactly what she'd wanted to say to Donovan. She knew she needed to clear the air, to be open and honest and tell him about

Carina's involvement in putting them together. That had been her intent when she and Carina had come earlier, meeting his brother instead. She'd known since that first day that for them to move forward, there could be no secrets between them. Donovan needed to know the truth. Now she couldn't even think clearly, unable to remember the speech she'd been practicing in her head since they'd last parted.

Donovan stepping up behind her caused her to jump, startled out of her thoughts.

"You scared me," she snapped as she turned to face him.

He held up both hands as if he were surrendering. "I'm sorry. I didn't mean to frighten you."

They both took a collective breath and held it before either spoke again.

Donovan broke the silence. "So, what did you want…" he started, before suddenly noticing the horse standing off to the side.

The massive, bay-colored animal stood majestically, looking at them both as if he were waiting for something to happen. Even in the late-night darkness, there was no mistaking how exquisite the creature was with his rich, red-toned coloration and white stripe down the center of his face. Surprised, Donovan found himself staring as he and the horse eyed each other.

"His name's Raffaello," Gianna said as she moved to stroke the horse's snout.

"He's beautiful. What breed is he?" Donovan asked, moving closer to the animal, who gave him a subtle push with his nose. He brushed his hand against the horse's neck.

"He's a Maremmano. It's a local Tuscan breed."

"You rode over?"

Gianna nodded. "It was too dark to walk, and I didn't want to drive. I needed to think."

Donovan shifted his gaze to meet hers, nodding in understanding. He took another deep breath. "So, what did you want to talk about?"

Gianna hesitated, and then she shook her head as she shrugged her shoulders. "Do you want to ride?" she suddenly asked.

Before he could respond, she swung her body up onto the horse's back, nothing between her and the animal but a soft cotton blanket. She extended her hand toward him.

Donovan paused for just a brief moment. "What's his name again?" he asked.

"Raffaello."

"After the painter?"

She laughed. "No, the turtle."

Confusion washed over Donovan's face. "The turtle?"

Gianna laughed again. "The Teenage Mutant Ninja Turtles."

Donovan was still staring at her as if she'd lost her mind.

A huge grin crossed her face. "There's Leonardo, Donatello, Michelangelo and Raphael. You really don't know your pop culture!"

He shrugged his broad shoulders. "Something you'll need to teach me."

"Carina and I named all the horses after them."

"All the horses?"

"We have six."

"And the other two are named?"

"Hermione and Ginevra—Ginny for short."

Donovan paused. "Harry Potter! I know those!" he said with a deep chuckle.

Gianna laughed with him. "That was all Carina's idea. I'm not a Harry Potter fan."

"But you like the turtle things?"

"I *love* the turtle things!" She waved her hand. "So, are you coming or not?"

Donovan took a deep breath as he clutched her arm and jumped, swinging the bulk of his body onto the horse's back behind her.

The beast beneath them neighed in response, twisting his head just enough to glare at the two of them. Gianna caressed the side of his thick neck. "Good boy!" she said. "Good boy!"

Once he was settled comfortably atop the animal, Donovan rested his hands lightly against her sides. Gianna grabbed one hand and then the other, pulling his arms closer around her waist.

"You'll need to hold on," she said, her words lost in the air as the horse started at a brisk gallop. "Hold on tight!"

Just the hint of a breeze was blowing as they rode beneath the late-night sky. Donovan's body was nestled close to Gianna's, her back leaning easily against his chest. Above their heads, stars shimmered brightly against the dark canvas, lighting their path. Everything about the moment felt surreal, and Donovan was awed by how at ease they both were.

He was completely lost as she navigated their way through the countryside, coming to a halt as they reached the coastline and the pristine Blue Flag beaches so popular with tourists. She led them to a secluded cove, then slid like a nymph from the horse's back and out of Donovan's arms. She left him sitting atop Raffaello as she skipped toward the expanse of warm, shallow water. Donovan watched as she kicked off her shoes, dipping her feet into the warm waters that lapped at the edge of the sand.

There was something exquisite about Gianna as she danced beneath the full moon, her thick waves loose and whipping over her shoulders. She was braless, wearing a simple tank top that amplified her small bustline. Her nipples had blossomed against the cotton fabric and pressed teasingly for attention. Boy-cut shorts complemented her well-rounded backside, her buttocks tight and firm like two generous-sized melons. She was lean, and despite her petite stature, her legs seemed to be a mile high. He suddenly imagined her in his arms, pressed against him, his hands trailing the lines and curves of her body. As if she were reading his mind, she suddenly turned and stared in his direction, wrapping her arms around her torso.

Donovan gently caressed the horse's side. "Easy boy," he said softly. "Easy."

Raffaello lifted his head and whinnied, the tone low

and gentle, as if he were encouraging Donovan to catch up to the woman.

The man chuckled softly as he dismounted. He gave the horse an easy hug. "Give me a break, big guy. She's a hard one to keep up with," he said out loud. The horse lifted his head again as though he were cosigning Donovan's statement.

A full moon reflected off the water, casting a glow around the landscape. As Donovan moved in Gianna's direction, she stared, turning to watch him. When he was close enough for the sea spray to kiss his face, she turned back and continued to walk, kicking up water beneath her feet. Donovan followed behind her, his arms crossed over his chest and his hands clutched tightly beneath his armpits.

"You look nervous," she said, coming to an abrupt stop as she turned again to face him.

He shook his head. "No. I'm just curious. Wondering what we're doing here in the middle of the night."

"I wanted to show you this place. It's one of my favorites. I come here and walk the sand when I need to figure something out."

"What are you trying to figure out?"

"*Our* story," she said emphasizing the word *our*. "Whether or not the hero gets the girl."

Donovan smiled ever so slightly. "The hero *always* gets the girl."

She smiled with him. "Not in my books."

"But you don't write romance."

"I don't. I've never really believed in happily-ever-after."

"Do you believe in the girl at least giving the hero a chance?"

Gianna took a breath, blowing it out slowly. "I do, but our story is different."

"Different how?"

Gianna suddenly changed the subject. "Do you smell that?" she asked, tilting her face upward as she inhaled deeply.

Donovan took his own deep inhale, noting the faintest hint of floral sweet that tinted the ocean air. He nodded.

"It's Italian jasmine," she responded. "It's still blooming, and it's late for this time of year. That's a good omen."

Donovan took a step toward her, closing the gap between them. "How is *our* story different, Gianna?"

She met the intense look he was giving her, hesitating for a split second before answering. "The heroine wasn't in it from the beginning. Only the hero."

Donovan stared at her, her comment spinning in his mind. His gaze dropped to the ground, flitting back and forth as he tried to make sense of her statement. When he lifted his eyes back to her face, she was gnawing nervously on her bottom lip.

She continued. "Carina was the one who initially reached out to you. Pretending to be me."

"Carina?"

Gianna nodded. "She wanted to fix us up. Her methods were just a little wayward."

"So it wasn't you who's been writing to me all these months?"

Gianna shook her head. "No. I only found out about you a few weeks before you arrived."

"So this whole time, all of this has been a game?" He suddenly thought back to the conversation with Kendrick and Graham and how the twins liked to play tricks on people.

"No! Not at all," she said emphatically. "Carina just wanted us to get to know each other. But everything she wrote, or rather what she sent you…those were all my words, my feelings. She took the writings from my personal journals to respond to you. And I've read every word you wrote me. I could probably recite them verbatim. Her responses would have been exactly what I would have said to you."

Donovan drew his hand over the top of his head and down his face. "No wonder you've been so…" He paused.

"I didn't want you to be hurt by this. I know you've been invested in our relationship far longer than I have, but I assure you, even though I've been playing catch up, you and I…"

He cut her words off, his tone harsh. "You and I don't have a relationship. You and your sister have been playing me for a fool," he said. "I can't believe after all this time that I didn't figure it out."

"I'm so sorry, Donovan," Gianna said, contrition in her eyes. "I really am. I needed to apologize. And I needed you to know the truth."

"Now you want me to know the truth? Why didn't you just tell me when we first met?"

Gianna eased even closer to him. She pressed her

palms to his chest, her fingers clutching the front of his shirt. "That very first day I wanted to, but once I met you... I...well... I really wanted to get to know you better. Carina and I had even planned to tell you earlier today, but when we got to your home and your brother was there, I changed my mind again."

"What difference does it make now?"

She took a deep breath and held it for a brief second. Donovan shook his head, moving to turn from her.

Gianna grabbed his arm, spinning herself back to stand in front of him. "Because when I do this," she whispered, "you need to know that it comes from me. From my heart."

Donovan's brow furrowed with confusion again. "When you do what?" he snapped.

Gianna closed what little space remained between them, pressing the warmth of her body to his. "This," she whispered softly as she stood on her tiptoes, tilting her face to his. And then she kissed him, capturing his mouth with her own.

Had he been asked, Donovan would have sworn on everything he held sacred that when Gianna kissed him, fireworks erupted in the sky and a symphony was playing blissfully in the distance. In his mind's eye he would have bet his last dollar that he'd seen the colorful striations connecting the bright stars above and that he'd heard the music that had danced with the lull of the waves that teased the sand.

He had never before been kissed as passionately as when her mouth blessed his. Her lips were soft, satin pillows. They parted slightly, her tongue playfully teasing his. It was an easy give-and-take of magnanimous proportions fueled by something too sweet to ever be believed. It was the best first kiss of all the first kisses in his small world.

As his lips danced over hers, she wrapped her thin arms around his neck, drawing him so close to her that it felt as if they were one body and not two. Her soft curves melded into every hardened line of his body, and neither could begin to decipher where one began and the other ended.

Donovan wrapped his arms around her waist, lifting her from the sandy foundation beneath her feet. As he did, she wrapped both legs around his waist, locking her ankles together at the small of his back. He clutched the round of her backside with one hand, his fingers teasing the taut flesh as the other skated up and down her torso.

The moment was surreal. Gianna was so lost in the vastness of it that when Donovan broke the connection, pushing her gently from him, the infraction felt magnanimous. They were both breathing heavily, gasping for air as he eased her back onto her feet and took a step from her, putting what she thought was far too much distance between them.

Donovan's head bobbed up and down against his neck, his mind racing with too many thoughts, but there was something in his eyes Gianna had never seen before. He reached a hand out, trailing his fingers along her profile as she closed her own eyes and leaned her cheek into his palm. When she reopened her eyes, Donovan was still staring, his gaze misted with emotion.

"I'll find my own way home," he said softly, the comment not at all what Gianna had expected.

"Donovan, please," she whispered back, clutching a hand to her chest. "Let's just talk."

He shook his head as he took two additional steps backward. "I'm sorry, Gianna, but I don't have anything else to say," he replied. And then he turned and disappeared into the darkness.

Chapter 8

Donovan stared out at the students who were taking their first exam of the semester. The surprise pop quiz was solely for his benefit, to assess the capabilities of his students and identify those mathematical areas where he needed to focus more energy and those he could dismiss. As he eyed each student, he was surprised to find Alessandra Donati staring back at him intently. The young woman slowly licked her lips just as she drew her number two pencil to her mouth, then gave him a suggestive wink. The overt gesture threw Donovan off course for a brief moment as he shifted his eye to the paperwork on his desk, pretending not to have noticed.

He took a deep breath before returning his gaze to the rows of seats and the thirty-six students sitting in them. He resumed his study of the classroom, starting his trek on the other side of the room. They were a great group, eager, inquisitive and bright. They would make the teaching experience a joy. Then there was young Ms. Donati, her flirtatious manner beginning to cause him concern.

The girl was intellectually gifted, but she had no boundaries. Her brazen antics since the semester had started went far above and beyond those of students he'd had in the past. And in the past, there had been many a student who'd hoped to know him outside of the classroom on a more intimate level, but Donovan had always been able to shut them down.

Shutting down Ms. Donati was proving to be a challenge. The first day of classes, she'd made her interest in him known in front of the whole class, the sexual innuendo making him blush a time or two. He'd pulled her aside immediately after class to express his disapproval, and she had only laughed, pretending not to know what he was talking about as she trailed her hands over her full breasts, drawing attention to the large nipples that poked through the sheer fabric. But the overt comments had since stopped, at least when there were others around to hear.

As the clock chimed through the room signaling the noon hour, Donovan moved onto his feet, collecting the exam papers as each student passed by his desk toward the exit. He wished them each a good afternoon as comments rang out about the ease or difficulty of the test.

"I wasn't prepared for that, Dr. Boudreaux!" one young man said, laughing.

"That was a breeze, sir!" another interjected. "You'll have to do better challenging us!"

Ms. Donati brought up the rear, hanging back to be the last to leave, as she did after every class. Before she could comment, her wide eyes showing her eagerness to whisper out of turn, Professor Mugabe burst through the door.

"Donovan, how was class? Oh, Alessandra, dear, how are you?"

The student shrugged her narrow shoulders, annoyance visible across her face. "I'm well, thank you," she answered.

There was a brief pause as the two instructors stood staring at the girl.

Alessandra shifted her gaze toward Donovan. "Professor Boudreaux, will you be having office hours today?" she asked as she twisted the beads around her neck between her fingers. "I'd like to speak to you, if I may? Alone."

Donovan shook his head. "I'll be in early tomorrow. In the common area until ten. You're more than welcome to come see me then," he answered, his eyebrows lifted ever so slightly.

She forced a smile. "Tomorrow then," she said as she sashayed out the door.

Professor Mugabe looked from him to Alessandra and back.

"You'll need to keep an eye on that one," she said as Alessandra disappeared from sight. "She's one of our best and brightest but…" The woman's words stalled. She pressed a hand to Donovan's forearm. "But I'm sure you've already figured that out." She gave him an all-knowing smile before she continued. "Do you have plans for lunch?"

"I was actually planning to just head home early since I don't have a class this afternoon." His brow furrowed, something else obviously on his mind.

"Nonsense!" Sophie exclaimed. "You must have lunch with me. We really haven't had an opportunity to talk since you got here." She headed for the door, calling over her shoulder, "I insist!"

Gianna entered the family home, a blank expression across her face. Carina and her father exchanged a look as she and Franco both turned to stare at the same time.

"Ciao, bambina!" the patriarch called out, gesturing for his daughter to come to his side.

Gianna crossed to the other side of the room, leaning in to kiss her father's cheek. *"Ciao, papà,"* she replied.

"Where were you?"

She shook her head. "I just went for a walk. No place special," she answered.

The old man nodded. "Have you spoken to Donovan?"

Gianna took a deep breath and sighed softly. She turned abruptly, not bothering to answer.

"You should try to call him, Sissy!" Carina called after her. "If you want I can try…"

Gianna turned to give her sister a look, cutting off the comment. "Leave it alone, Carina. You have helped more than enough," she said sarcastically.

Franco moved onto his feet, crossing to stand by her

side. "Carina is right. You two need to talk. You should try to call him."

She shook her head. "Donovan has made it quite clear that he isn't interested in talking to me, so let it go. Please."

Gianna stepped into her father's outstretched arms. Franco wrapped his daughter in a warm hug. He held her, no one saying another word. As she stood in his arms, she could feel the hurt that consumed her flooding her spirit, building yet again.

It had been a few weeks since she'd told Donovan the truth, and since then a wall of silence had stood like stone between the couple. All of the family had wanted to intervene, but Gianna had been adamant about none of them doing anything at all. It was over, no possibility of a future between them existing. Gianna had accepted such, and everyone else just needed to, as well.

Franco gave her a quick squeeze before kissing her cheek one last time and letting her go. Turning from him, Gianna moved toward her office, leaving them behind. Before she could close the door, Carina moved into the space.

"Please don't start," Gianna muttered. She swiped at a tear that burned hot behind her lashes.

"I just wanted you to know that I haven't gotten to your mail or your email messages yet. If you want me to, I can take care of them now."

Gianna shook her head. "No, I'll take care of it. I have some calls to make, too. If I need anything, I'll just let you know."

"You're pushing your deadline. How's the writing going?"

Gianna paused. Truth be told, she hadn't written a word since that last night with Donovan, her mind a complete and total blank. The writing wasn't going well at all. She forced a smile as she met her sister's stare. "Fine. The writing is going very well."

"So, you'll make your deadline? Because if you don't think you will, we should send your editor a message."

"I said it's going to be okay, Carina. I'm handling it."

Carina nodded. "Well, let me know if that changes, okay?"

"Okay, Carina!" Gianna snapped.

An awkward silence fell between them. Carina said nothing else as she backed her way out of the office, closing the door behind her.

Gianna sat down at her desk, then flung the felt-tip pen she'd been holding across the room, the device landing in front of the wooden bookcases. She shifted forward in her seat, dropping her head into her hands. Frustration creased her brow.

Nothing felt as if it was going to be okay. She felt lost and couldn't begin to explain to anyone why. Donovan turning from her had broken her heart, and she couldn't begin to know or understand when her heart had gotten caught up in the fray. And then she thought about that first kiss.

Kissing Donovan Boudreaux had been everything she'd imagined and then some. The man's touch had been searing, and in that brief moment, when their connection had been the most intimate experience of her life, Gianna had imagined her fairy-tale romance and happy ending. Nothing about how he held her, his body pressed tightly against hers, had prepared her for that being their very last kiss. Nothing. But that's where they were. Done and finished before anything had been able to start.

Shaking the thoughts from her head, Gianna turned on her computer. As she waited for the device to power up, she eased her headphones over her ears and flipped the on switch to her MP3 player. The English crooner Sam Smith was suddenly serenading her, his melodic tone instantly calming her spirit. He sang, and Gianna allowed herself to drift into the emotion of his tune.

She slid her finger across the laptop's mouse pad, opening her email folder. After entering her user name and password, she watched as a lengthy list of new messages rolled across the screen. She scanned the names beneath the list titled FROM. One name suddenly screamed for her attention. As she clicked on the message, a bright smile pulled at her lips, joy flooding her face. She read it once and then again.

Dear Ms. Martelli,
My name is Donovan Boudreaux. I'm a math profes-sor currently teaching at the University of Siena in Tus-cany. I have been a fan of yours since your first book, *Bruised and Battered*. Despite my previous intentions to write and tell you how much I've enjoyed your writ-ing, I've always stopped myself, feeling that you proba-bly would not want to be inundated with more fan mail. But I have been reading an ARC of your latest work,

Primed and Pursued, and have been so engaged with the characters that I could not let the opportunity to tell you what I think pass by.

I am awed by the beauty of your words. From the first sentence to the last, I was pulled in and captivated. But I was also haunted, your protagonist's pain seeming to mirror my own. So I had to write to ask if his heartbreak was intentional on your part or just a consequence of your heroine's actions. I'd be curious to know as well if you ever considered rewriting the ending to mend the hurt the infraction caused him. Clearly, you had compassion for this man, so does he not deserve a happier ending?

I'd love to discuss him and your story in further detail. I do hope that you'll respond.

Yours truly,

Donovan Boudreaux

Excitement bubbled like boiling water in a pot as Gianna grabbed an ink pen and yellow-lined notepad from the corner of her desk. As a response formed in her mind, she began jotting down notes, anxious to send a reply.

As Sophie prattled on and on about testing and student scores, Donovan found himself drifting off into his own thoughts. The woman had been talking nonstop since they'd taken a seat at the sidewalk trattoria. He'd given up trying to get in a comment and resigned himself to just listening, occasionally nodding in agreement.

The meal had been a delight—appetizers of classic

caprese salad with tomatoes and buffalo mozzarella cheese, and Tuscan prosciutto with cantaloupe melon. He'd chosen saffron risotto with veal *ossobuco* ragout for his main course, and had finished off with a scoop of mango sorbet in a bowl of raspberry soup.

Now he sat clutching his smartphone in his lap, hoping for the distinctive sound that alerted him to an incoming email message. Before leaving home, he'd sent Gianna an email, hoping against all odds to start their relationship over again. For days he'd stopped himself from climbing that hill to the winery to see her, wanting to forget that he'd left her and her horse standing alone on the beach in the dark of night. And as often as the thought of seeing her came to him, he'd talked himself out of it, able to forgive but unable to forget that she and her sister had played him for a fool.

But this morning had started differently than all the other mornings. Signora Rossi had wakened him as usual, her boisterous chatter like its own alarm clock on the other side of his bedroom door. The old woman had knocked for his attention, and when he'd finally wrapped a bathrobe around himself to greet her, she'd been in an exceptional mood.

Pushing him out of her way, he'd watched as she stripped the sheets from his bed, and then out of nowhere she'd reached into his nightstand drawer and had pulled Gianna's framed picture from where he'd hidden it inside. Propping it back onto the tabletop, Signora Rossi had given him an evil eye and had shaken her index finger at him as she'd berated him in her native tongue. He'd understood just enough to know that she thought him a bigger fool for allowing the rift between them to continue. And so he'd given in to his wanting and had gone to his computer to send Gianna a message.

Sophie interrupted his thoughts. "Maybe we can have dinner together tomorrow?"

"Excuse me?" He struggled to focus his attention back on Sophie, shaking the thoughts of Gianna from his mind.

"Dinner? Tomorrow? I was thinking that you could come to my apartment and I could cook a traditional Nigerian meal for you." Sophie smiled brightly, her porcelain white teeth a striking contrast against her dark complexion.

As Donovan stared into the woman's eyes, he realized something between them had changed, Sophie reading more into their friendship than he'd ever considered.

"I'm sorry," he said. He repeated himself a second time. "I'm really sorry, but…"

She held up her hands, her smile still bright. "No pressure. I just sense that you've been off your game lately, and I thought some downtime with a good friend might help alleviate some of your stress. So think about it, and if you change your mind or you just feel like spending some time together, I'm available."

Donovan nodded. "I appreciate that," he said, feeling extremely uncomfortable.

His phone suddenly vibrated. As he stole a quick glance to see who the incoming message was from, Sophie changed the subject, telling him about her family and the journey from Africa that had landed them on the Italian coast. Despite wanting to focus his attention on his phone, he instead leaned toward Sophie to hear the story she was so excited to share. The message from his sister could wait. He wouldn't be rude to the woman who was trying so hard to be a good friend.

An hour later, he stole a quick glance at his wristwatch. Half the afternoon had passed, and he found himself wishing he were anywhere but where he was. He moved as if to ready himself to leave.

"Don't rush off," Sophie said as she shifted in her seat. "It's still early. We could order a bottle of wine, maybe take a stroll through the piazza?"

He smiled. "I appreciate the invitation, Sophie. I really do, but I have to head back to Maremma."

She nodded. "I'm glad we could spend some time together." She reached across the table for his hand. "I'm really glad that we're getting to know each other better. You know how much I've always admired you."

"Sophie…look…"

She interrupted, batting her eyelashes at him. "Donovan, I'm really not good at this kind of thing, but I like you and you like me, and we have so much in common. I feel like we could have more with each other. I know you feel it, too!"

His palm was sweaty as she caressed his fingers, a look of longing in her dark eyes. Extricating himself from her touch, he shifted backward in his seat, dropping both of his hands into his lap. "Sophie, I'm sorry. I hope I didn't give you the wrong impression but…"

"But you're lonely and you crave companionship and a woman's touch in your life. I see it in your eyes, and the past few weeks in particular I've felt like you've been missing something."

He shook his head vehemently as he stammered. "I was… I mean… I am… I don't…" He took a deep breath, his two hands suddenly gesturing in the air as he tried to explain himself. "I have had a lot on my mind lately, but it's not what you think. I appreciate everything you've done for me, but I don't want to give you the impression that you and I are anything but friends. Good friends. And colleagues! But that's all we are."

"Aren't you attracted to me? Because I'm very attracted to you, Donovan. I think you know that. And we're so at ease with each other!"

Donovan took a deep breath. "You're a beautiful woman, Sophie! There's no doubt about that, but I'm just not…"

"Is there someone else? Because if there's someone else, you should have told me!"

Donovan felt the woman bristle with indignation. He shook his head. "It really doesn't matter! What matters is that I hope you and I can continue to be friends. I do value our friendship, and I enjoy working with you. I wouldn't want to see anything happen to that friendship because of a misunderstanding."

Sophie sat staring at him, the glare in her eyes shifting to something cold. "Well, don't I feel silly," she said. "I'm completely embarrassed. I can't believe I just threw myself at you like that, just to have you shoot me down."

"Don't be," he said, shaking his head. "And I didn't shoot you down. Don't think like that. We're just on different pages right now. Maybe some other time, some other place, things would have been different. But I'm a man. Always a day late and a dollar short when it comes to women!" Donovan tried to laugh it off to ease her discomfort. But Sophie wasn't feeling it.

Silence swelled thick between them. He suddenly felt even more awkward than he had before. He moved onto his feet, practically jumping out of his seat. "Thank you for lunch…and the company. I had a good time. And again, I'm really sorry if I gave you the wrong impression."

Sophie shrugged, fighting not to let her embarrassment flood her face. "Have a good night," she muttered as she waved a dismissive hand.

Donovan moved to the other side of the table. He dropped a heavy hand against the woman's shoulder. She turned her head, leaning to search the interior of her handbag. When she didn't bother to look at him again, he gave her shoulder a slight squeeze as he said goodbye. Heading in the direction of his car, Donovan suddenly wished he could run, not walk, from the woman's sight.

His hour-long ride home to Maremma helped ease the anxiety that had afflicted the last few minutes of his time with Sophie. He thought about her and about Alessandra—both women had put him in an awkward position. Although it wasn't the first time someone had expressed interest in him, Donovan had avoided commitment by throwing himself into his work. Not many women readily accepted taking a backseat to a man's profession. But he instinctively knew that the few he had dated were not the partners he was meant to spend his life with. And then Gianna had come along.

He accelerated the car, frustrated by the limited cell service in the area. Before pulling out of the restaurant's parking lot he'd checked his phone, but there had been no message from the woman. He was hoping that once he got closer to home and a better signal that Gianna might have finally responded to his message.

Chapter 9

Donovan caught sight of Raffaello as he pulled his car in front of the cottage. The horse was grazing out in the fields, seemingly oblivious to his surroundings. Donovan's heart began to race with excitement as he stepped out of his car. Then he heard the two women bickering. Gianna and Signora Rossi sounded like two cats trapped in a burlap bag. His heart skipped a beat, and then a second one. As he neared the front door of his home, he stopped to listen, able to understand more of the language than he'd anticipated.

Signora Rossi was fussing about pasta and how it needed to be hand-formed. Gianna said something about her father and having perfected his methods of pulling the dough through a pasta machine. One of them mentioned watching Mario Batali and how he did it on television, and then the raised voices sniped at each other again like nails against a chalkboard.

Amusement painted Donovan's face as he stepped through the entrance into the house. He looked from one woman to the other, then settled his gaze on Gianna's face. The two stood in the center of his kitchen, flour dusting Gianna's face as she took direction from Signora Rossi. Startled, both women jumped in surprise.

"Hi," Donovan said, his eyes locking with Gianna's. He stood staring, something large and magnanimous shifting between them as they eyed each other.

"Ciao!" she replied, a warm smile pulling at her thin lips.

Signora Rossi grinned as her own gaze shifted between them. "You are early!" she said, speaking English to him for the very first time.

His eyes widened in surprise, but before he could respond the old woman rushed him, fanning her hand for him to get out of their way.

He and Gianna both laughed.

"I wanted to surprise you with dinner," Gianna said. "But it seems like I don't know what I'm doing!"

He nodded. "I guess I'll go into the other room until you two are done," he said, locking gazes with her a second time.

She nodded. "Read your mail," she said as he moved toward the bedroom.

Tossing her a quick glance over his shoulder, he smiled, a huge grin filling his face as he shut the room door between them. As soon as it was closed, the back-and-forth between the two women began again, Signora Rossi admonishing Gianna for not having his meal ready when he came through the door. Donovan couldn't help but laugh.

A legal-sized envelope rested in the center of the bed. Donovan took a seat against the mattress as he pulled it into his hands and opened the seal. The letter inside was handwritten, dark ink staining two pages of bright white copy paper. Shifting his large body back against the headboard, Donovan began to read.

My dearest Donovan,
I've drafted this response more times than I care to count, and just when I thought I was ready to push the send button on my computer, I hesitated. What if you thought the response came from someone other than me? The fear of you not trusting that these words were mine was haunting! Letter writing has become a lost art, but I knew that it needed to be revived between us, and so I put pen to paper.

Your support of my writing warms my heart. And to have your friendship means the world to me. But you are more than just a friend, and I haven't even begun to show you just how much more you mean to me.

So to answer your question, no, it was never my intention to break my hero's heart. He is *my* hero! The alpha of *my* story! But he is also a man, and the circumstances of the story and the actions of those he could not control proved to be his undoing. But he is *my* hero! And I lay claim

to him because he has my heart and is everything
I could ever want in a man. Even as he fell, there
was no denying his strength, his unyielding abil-
ity to rise like the phoenix to fly again! So there
was no need to rewrite his ending, because even
in his hurt, there was hope and a heroine's love
to pull him from the ashes!

Hope! And love! The words of a romantic!
Something I knew nothing of...until you.
PS: I would give anything to have you kiss me
again like you kissed me that very first time! I
just thought I would share that with you.

Donovan reread the letter again before tucking it between the pages of his Bible and putting the book on the
nightstand. In the other room, laughter rang warmly,
even as the clatter of pots and pans vibrated through
the air.

Donovan and Gianna talked over bowls of linguine
tossed with artichokes, Roma tomatoes and fresh Par-
mesan cheese. They washed the meal down with a bottle
of white wine, then finished it off with slices of tira-
misu and cups of dark coffee topped with steamed milk.
They talked for hours, falling easily into a comfortable
rhythm with each other.

Outside, Gianna's horse slumbered on his feet. After
clearing the dirty dishes, the young woman rose to
check on the animal. Before she returned, she stopped
to call her father so that he would not worry about where
she was. She wasn't surprised to learn that the village

gossips had already carried the news, everyone whispering about her and the handsome professor. Then she'd called her sister. Carina had cried with excitement, moving Gianna to shed her own tears of joy.

Back inside, there was a lull in the conversation as both took sips of their hot beverage. Gianna rested her gaze on Donovan's face. The emotion that suddenly flooded her spirit was unexpected. Being back with him felt surreal, and she imagined that it would be devastating if she suddenly found herself waking from the sweetest dream. As if he were reading her mind, Donovan smiled.

"I'm sorry," she said, her voice a loud whisper. "I hope that you know that Carina only wanted the best for both of us. I should have told you the truth the minute I found out what she had done, and I apologize for not doing so."

"I do know that, but my feelings were hurt. I felt deceived. Hell, I was deceived! And I didn't understand why you just weren't honest with me." He leaned toward her, dropping his forearms against his thighs as he stared, his hands clasped tightly together.

A hint of a blush crossed her face. She took a deep breath, blowing it out slowly before she responded. "After I read all the messages you'd sent, I really did want to get to know you. I was curious. Then when we met…well… I thought you were the most beautiful man I'd ever laid eyes on. And one of the sweetest. Once I felt like we'd connected, I didn't think it would matter. So, no, I'm not going to apologize for how I felt, but I'm sincerely apologetic for not being transparent."

He nodded. "What made you change your mind?"

"I didn't want our relationship to be built on a lie. You wanted more from me, and when I realized that I did, too, I felt like I owed it to you to be honest."

His head continued to bob up and down as he reflected on what she had to say. "So you wanted more?"

Gianna scooted her chair against his, easing herself closer. She clasped his hands between her own and pressed a kiss against his palm. She shook her head. "No."

Donovan suddenly looked confused. "No?"

She smiled. "I *want* more. There's nothing past tense about what I feel for you, Donovan Boudreaux! Or what I hope will happen between us."

Donovan smiled. Just as he leaned forward, his face mere millimeters from hers, there was a hard rap at his front door. Before either could stand to answer, the door flew open and Signora Rossi pushed her way inside. She took one look at the two of them and tossed up her hands, her thick accent ringing in the air as she scurried to clean up the dirty dishes.

Gianna leaned forward and kissed Donovan's cheek. She brushed her own against the stubble of new growth that had sprouted across his face. Donovan blew a frustrated breath of air past her ear.

"I should be leaving," she said. "It's past your curfew."

"I was hoping you could stay," he whispered, cutting an eye at the old woman who was pretending not to notice them.

"We're not ready for that yet," Gianna answered as she stood, her smile endearing.

Donovan stood with her and slowly walked her toward the sliding glass doors to the rear patio.

Signora Rossi called out from the other side of the room. *"Dille buonanotte. È necessario il riposo."*

Donovan's eyes widened. "Did she just say that I needed my rest?" he muttered.

Gianna giggled. "And she told you to tell me goodnight so you could get that rest."

"Dille buonanotte!" Signora Rossi repeated, waving a wooden spoon at the two of them.

Donovan shook his head, his smile miles wide as Gianna drew her hand along his profile in a gentle caress. There was no denying the wealth of emotion between them. Donovan suddenly imagined that they had a lifetime of loving to carry them forward. Because in that moment, he could have easily said, without an ounce of reservation, that he had fallen head over heels in love with Gianna Martelli. He knew beyond any doubt that he would spend a lifetime ensuring she and everyone else knew it. Those few weeks apart had been telling, and devastating, and he refused to be away from her that long ever again.

He pressed his forehead to hers, his eyes closed as he held her tightly. When he opened them, every ounce of emotion he was feeling was mirrored in her eyes. She smiled, joy and happiness shimmering in her stare. Donovan suddenly wanted to kiss her.

As if reading his mind, Gianna gently pressed her closed lips to his, the touch sweet and easy, like the delicate touch of butterfly wings against a blade of summer grass. Donovan felt his heart stop and then start again, and a level of calm washed over them both. Perfection didn't begin to describe the moment between them.

"Good night," she said softly.

Donovan nodded. "Good night, Gianna!"

And Signora Rossi had the last word, wishing them both a very good night. *"Buonanotte!"*

Mason, Kendrick, Guy and Darryl were all laughing into their telephones as the Boudreaux brothers caught up with Donovan via a conference call.

"That's taking blocking to a whole other level!" Guy said.

Donovan nodded, his gaze focused on the road as he talked with his earpiece in place. "I thought our sisters were bad," he said, "but they've got nothing on Signora Rossi!"

"But it sounds like things are good with you and Gianna, yes?" Kendrick asked.

"I think we're on the right path. We're talking, and things are comfortable between us."

"That's good," Kendrick said, "because the woman is beautiful. I don't think you can do any better than that."

Donovan laughed. "Excuse me?"

His brothers all laughed.

"I've seen a picture," Guy added. "Kendrick might be right."

Mason spoke. "As long as it feels right and you're happy, that's all that matters. Have you spoken to the old people?"

"Dad called the other day, and I was planning to call Mom after my morning class today."

"Make sure you do that. Mom is missing you. And she's had a lot to say about you and your new friend. The rest of us are tired of hearing it, so this will give her a chance to tell you directly."

Darryl laughed. "Mom's not missing him! She's hoping he'll be married with a child on the way by the time he gets back from Italy."

"That may be true," Mason said in agreement, "but she needs to tell him and not us."

"And he might not come back from Italy," Kendrick interjected.

There was a brief pause before Mason broke the silence. "Are you thinking about staying in Italy?" he asked.

Donovan took a deep breath. "I don't see Gianna wanting to leave."

There was a collective sigh from all the brothers.

Kendrick laughed. "Please, please, please! Have a wedding so your sisters will have something to focus on. I need them to leave me and Vanessa alone!"

"Just let them give you a damn party and get it over with!" Guy exclaimed. "That's all they want to do!"

Mason agreed. "They're all still pissed that you eloped. Since they couldn't get a wedding, and Vanessa's school schedule is keeping them from throwing you guys a reception to celebrate, they're chomping at the bit!"

The siblings all laughed as the banter between them continued. By the time Donovan pulled into his parking lot at the university, he'd laughed until tears spilled out of his eyes.

"I've got to go," he said as he shut off the car. "I'll give you a guys a call in a few days."

"Full day today?" Mason asked.

"No. I only have office hours this morning, then I'm done for the weekend."

"I have to come back for business in a few weeks," Kendrick said. "Let's plan on doing dinner."

"I think I might come with him," Mason said.

"I think we should all go. Make it a guy's trip," Guy said.

"I'm in!" Darryl chimed.

Donovan cosigned. "Sounds like a plan!"

After saying their goodbyes, he disconnected the call and headed for the entrance. Accustomed to Sophie meeting him at the door, he was only slightly surprised to not see her standing there. After grabbing his mail from the boxes in the office, he headed for the common area to fulfill his office hours and be available to his students.

Donovan favored the out-of-office environment and had discovered over the years that many of his students preferred to seek him out in an open area instead of behind closed doors. A public environment also made things easier when dealing with students like Alessandra.

She sat waiting, like a stalker, desperate to seek him out. Pacing the floors, she almost jumped with joy as he moved in her direction. "Dr. Boudreaux, I thought you forgot about me."

He smiled politely. "Why would you think something like that?"

She looked at her watch, then lifted her eyes back

to his. "I guess I am a little early," she said with a soft giggle.

Donovan nodded. "Thirty minutes early, to be exact." He gestured for her to take a seat at the table, pulling out a chair for her. "So, what can I help you with, Ms. Donati?"

Alessandra fumbled her books and bags as she twisted in her seat to face him. "I just wanted to take an opportunity to personally welcome you to our university. Everyone is so excited to have you here."

He nodded, his eyebrows raised. "I appreciate that," he said slowly. "Is that it?"

She gave him a sly smile and curled her bottom lip as she bit down against the soft flesh. "I also wanted to volunteer to help you get settled in. I imagine being in a new country can be intimidating, especially when you don't know anyone. I want you to know that I'm at your disposal, day…or night," she said with emphasis. To further punctuate her meaning, she winked at him.

Donovan sat back in his seat, staring at her. He took a deep breath before he spoke. "That's very kind of you, Ms. Donati…"

"Please, Alessandra. Ms. Donati is so formal."

"Which is why I won't call you by your given name. There is nothing casual about our relationship. I'm your instructor and you are my student, and I have no intentions of crossing that line. Neither should you."

"But, Donovan…"

"Dr. Boudreaux. Please."

She bristled, twisting her mouth as annoyance flashed across her face. "Most men would welcome my attention," she snapped, her eyes narrowing into thin slits.

Donovan smiled. "Ms. Donati, I'm not like *most* men!"

Donovan watched as Alessandra stormed out of the common room, pausing once at the door to give him one last dirty look. As she made her exit, he missed her encounter in the hallway, the young woman almost slamming into Professor Mugabe. Nor was he privy to the subsequent conversation between the two. A conversation that had the two women whispering frantically until taking their discussion behind the closed doors of Professor Mugabe's office.

Before he could reflect on what had happened, another student waved for his attention, the young man in need of actual assistance with his math work. Two hours later he was wishing he could be done for the day, anxious to get back to Maremma, and Gianna. But there was still a mountain of paperwork that he needed to get through.

"Dr. Boudreaux?"

Donovan lifted his eyes from the stack of test papers he'd been grading. A young woman with doe-like eyes and a mousy pixie cut stood staring. She clutched a stack of books in her arms, the tomes almost as big as she was.

"Yes?" He eyed her curiously.

"You have a visitor in the front office. They asked me to come tell you."

"Grazie mille," he said, expressing his gratitude.

As she turned on high heels and headed toward a table of friends watching them curiously, he began to pack his papers into his leather attaché case. Minutes later he took his exit, heading in the direction of the university's reception area.

Gianna was standing in the office, her hands clasped together in front of her. Her eyes were darting back and forth as she took in the comings and goings of the students. She wore a blue skirt that was gathered on both sides and a blue-printed bandeau top that was tied into a bow between her breasts. Low cut, brown leather boots covered her feet, complementing her casual country look. She'd straightened her hair, the luscious strands falling well past her shoulders. He could feel a wide grin pull across his face at the sight of her spying into the glass-enclosed room.

As he moved in Gianna's direction, he was surprised when Sophie entered the office ahead of him and greeted her, the two women seeming to know one another. Neither seemed pleased to see the other, and he sensed their meeting was chilly at best. There was a brief exchange of words before Sophie did an about-face, slamming the door harshly as she made an exit. Moving in the opposite direction, she didn't see him, and for that he was grateful. He made a mental note to ask Gianna about their connection once they were alone.

She greeted him with a hug and a damp kiss to his cheek. "Donovan, *ciao!*"

"*Ciao*, Gianna! What brings you here?" he asked as he hugged her back.

"I came to steal you away. You don't have any classes this afternoon, right?"

Donovan nodded and smiled. "No, I don't. In fact, you caught me just in time. I was just about to head back to Maremma."

She grinned. "Then I'm glad I caught you."

Minutes later the couple was driving in a Mini Cooper convertible with the top down.

"Cute car," Donovan said as he threw an arm over the back of her seat. "Is this yours?"

"It's Carina and Graham's," she said. "I borrowed it so we could enjoy the sunshine." She tossed him a look and giggled. "There are some cars that large black men should never be seen in." She laughed.

Donovan laughed with her. "I assume a Mini Cooper is one of them?"

"That and a Volkswagen Beetle. The original ones!" She nodded as she took a narrow curb without slowing her speed. Donovan grabbed the dashboard to steady himself. His stomach jumped slightly.

"Hey, can you slow down?" he said, his voice raised.

Gianna laughed. "You're in safe hands, Donovan!" she said. "Very safe hands."

"I'm not so sure about that," he said as she took another curve without hitting brakes. He shook his head and laughed with her. "So where are we going?"

She gave him another look out of the corner of her eye. "The hot water springs!"

Chapter 10

The environment was relaxing and harmonious. Steam wafted off the surface of the thermal waters, the sulfurous spring nicely heated. The thermal waterfalls of Gorello were renowned for their therapeutic properties, immersion seeming to give healing and relaxation.

Donovan sat waist-deep in the open pools, his bare back against a rock formation, bathing in absolute tranquillity. Gianna sat beside him, her legs extended as she poked one foot and then another up above the warm waters. His hand rested against her upper thigh, gently kneading the soft skin, while hers caressed his forearm, a slow up and down stroke as her fingertips teased his flesh. Their gentle caresses were light and easy. The sensual exchange had them both heated, desire billowing in gusts as thick as the steam.

Donovan had read everything about the Tuscan region and he knew the science behind the geothermal activity underneath its surface, but to see it and experience the luxury was something else altogether. "This is wonderful," he murmured, his eyes closed as the waters flowed like a whirlpool around him. "This place has to be heaven-sent!"

Gianna nodded, leaning her head against his shoulders. "The old people will tell you that the springs were formed by lightning bolts thrown by the mythological deity Jupiter. During a violent quarrel with Saturn, the violent bolts thrown missed, causing the formations." She sat forward, turning to stare at him. "So the gods might have had something to do with it!"

Donovan chuckled. Opening his eyes, he met her stare. "Thank you," he said softly.

"For what?" she asked curiously.

"For this," he said as he leaned forward and pressed his mouth to hers.

Kissing Gianna had become his absolute favorite thing to do. The woman always tasted of peaches and honeysuckle, like the sweet Moscato blend that had become one of his favorite wines to indulge in. Her mouth was soft, a gentle cushion against his own, and at the first touch every nerve ending in his body fired with joy.

When he pulled away, breaking the connection, he was dazzled by the light that shimmered in her eyes and across her face. In that moment, everything was right in his small world. A tear suddenly misted at the edges of her eyes. His own widened, concern wafting across his face. "Baby, what's wrong?"

She shook her head. "Nothing. I'm just happy," she answered as she kissed him again. She moved onto her feet and held out her hand.

"So, where are we going now?" he asked as Gianna pulled him along behind her.

She threw him a quick look over her shoulder, the expression across her face saying everything Donovan needed to know.

As they pulled her car into the driveway, Signora Rossi stood in conversation with Signor D'Ascenzi and his wife, Pia. The three seniors were animated, laughing heartily. Their conversation came to a halt as they watched the couple exit the vehicle and move toward the door. Donovan and Gianna both waved heartily.

The two women cut their eyes at each other, all-knowing smirks across their faces. The two called Gianna's name, their tones sounding like admonishments, and the exchange between the three was quick and tense. But it was the hand gestures that gave away the tone of the conversation, a few overt and blatant.

Gianna tossed up her own hands as she laughed. *"Mamma mia,"* she muttered beneath her breath. She turned toward Donovan. "I'll wait for you inside," she whispered.

"Arrivederci!" she said as she gave them all a wave, professing that she had work she needed to finish.

The old man grinned, and Donovan felt himself blush ever so slightly as he and Gianna traded a look.

"It is good to see you again," Signor D'Ascenzi said.

Donovan shook his outstretched hand. "And you, too, sir!"

"My wife wanted to stop by and bring you some of her cookies," he said. "Signora Rossi put them on your counter."

"*Grazie!* I appreciate that."

The man gestured toward his wife. "Well, it's getting late and these two have been cackling like hens for over an hour now. My head needs a rest so I'm going home to put my feet up."

The two men shook hands one last time. "*Grazie*, Signora D'Ascenzi!" Donovan said as he leaned down to kiss first one cheek and then the other.

She said something in response and Signora Rossi laughed, the two women resuming their conversation. Donovan looked toward the other man for translation. Signor D'Ascenzi shook his head. "Those two say *la signorina* Martelli has kissed many frogs before finding herself a prince."

Donovan laughed as the man gestured for him to walk with him toward his truck. As they moved out of earshot, he gave Donovan a tap on the back and pointed toward the door Gianna had disappeared behind.

"She is a lot of woman, that one," he said approvingly, his voice a loud whisper. "And she doesn't look anything like a cow! So don't pay those two any mind. That one is a keeper!"

Donovan stood with Signora Rossi, the two watching as her guests disappeared down the road. He was suddenly conscious of the look the older woman was giving him, and then out of the blue she tapped him on his backside. His eyes widened in surprise.

"Non tenere una signora in attesa," she said as she pointed toward his front door before turning to her own unit and disappearing inside.

With a low chuckle, Donovan did what he was told and headed into his own space. The home was quiet save for the soft music that echoed out of the back bedroom. And dark, the only hint of light coming from the rear. A wave of nervous excitement suddenly flooded his spirit, moving him to shake in his shoes.

Gianna was sitting in the only chair in the room, a plush recliner newly upholstered in a soft brown fabric. She was barefoot, her shoes kicked off in the doorway and her legs pulled up beneath her buttocks. She sat with a yellow-lined notepad and an ink pen in her lap. As he entered, she looked up from the notes she was writing, meeting his dark gaze.

Donovan grinned, twisting his hands together anxiously.

"Finally got enough of their teasing?" Gianna asked.

He laughed. "They're definitely having fun at our expense. Signora Rossi just told me not to keep my lady waiting, then she goosed my left cheek and tapped my bottom."

Gianna laughed. "She's always been a little wild! After my mother died, she was a real help to my father. We fuss with each other, but I really do adore her."

"I get the impression she's fond of you, too."

The young woman gave him a slight shrug. The two exchanged glances, eyeing each other intently.

Donovan took a deep inhale of air, blowing it out slowly. "Would you like a glass of wine?" he asked, lifting the blanket of silence that had dropped between them.

She shook her head no as she let the notepad and pen slide to the floor. She moved onto her feet, saying nothing as she headed in the direction of his bathroom. With each step, she was coming out of her clothes, kicking off her skirt first and then pulling her top up and over her head.

In the doorway she turned, standing in nothing but a black lace G-string, the look in her eyes making her the perfect temptress. Her breasts were pert, standing at full attention. Her stomach was washboard flat, and there was just enough curve to her hips to give him pause. She slowly drew her hands through her hair, pulling the thick strands into a high topknot.

Stunned, Donovan felt his knees lock, his feet like lead weights against the hardwood floors. She looked delicious, and he found himself salivating with want. Every muscle in his body had hardened, each sinewy fiber like a rubber band pulled taut and ready to pop. With her boundaries and coyness nonexistent, he could do nothing but marvel at her boldness.

She crooked her finger and gestured. "Come wash my back," she said and then she turned, disappearing into the room.

Racing behind her, Donovan's own confidence never faltered as he dropped his pants, stepping out of them in the doorway. He pulled at his T-shirt, ripping the cotton fabric as she turned on the shower, pausing as the water warmed. The air around them had changed. The room was charged with excitement and a sensuality neither had experienced before. He moved swiftly to Gianna's side, brushing his finger across her bottom lip before capturing her mouth with his own, his hands sweeping in broad passes across her body.

Donovan kissed her lips, and then her neck, and the feel of his tongue on her skin made her breathing hitch, air catching deep in her chest. He gladly followed as she pulled him into the shower, dousing them both under the misted spray.

Gianna found herself wanting Donovan more than she had ever wanted anything or anyone before, and she suddenly questioned if she'd ever be able to tame the uncontrollable urges he'd suddenly stirred within her. She couldn't stop her heart from racing, the pounding beat thunderous as he began to kiss her breasts, suckling her nipples. He nibbled and teased the chocolate protrusions, making her moan as he licked around each hardened nub in turn, intensifying the wetness between her thighs.

The sweet spot between Gianna's legs throbbed, and the moist feeling exposed the yearnings and anticipation that suddenly consumed her. She was starved for Donovan's touch, and the craving was so intense she suddenly feared never coming back from the ecstasy she'd fallen into. Her desperation for more had suddenly become unbearable.

So lost in the warmth of each other, neither knew when or how they'd made it from the shower to Donovan's bed, the bedspread snatched away and strewn to the floor, the sheets damp from the moisture of their skin. They danced in perfect sync across the bed top, moving from corner to corner as they explored each other's bodies, gentle caresses followed by soft kisses. Both licked and nipped and teased and taunted the other until they were both breathing heavily, gasps and moans resounding through the room.

Gianna clasped the back of his head as his tongue explored her mouth, grazing the line of teeth as he playfully dueled with her tongue. His mouth trailed damp kisses up and down the length of her body, and then he paused, blowing warm breath against her inner thighs. His fingers teased the line of her intimate folds, her feminine moisture coating the tips. Her hips lifted off the bed, her body moving of its own volition as she pressed herself into his palm.

And then he tossed her a sexy smirk just before pressing his face between her legs, the intimate kiss causing her to cry out with pleasure. She clutched his ears as he reached for heaven with each decadent lick. It was more than she could bear as her body convulsed with pleasure, wave after wave of hedonistic delight exploding through every vein.

As she rode each swell, her emotions surging with a vengeance, Donovan quickly sheathed himself with a condom and entered her swiftly. He clutched her hair, his fingers tangled in the thick curls as he plunged his body into hers over and over again. His pace was rapid, each thrust of his hips harder and harder until she shouted his name over and over again into his chest.

Gianna screamed and Donovan screamed with her, muffling their cries as he pressed his mouth to hers. They orgasmed together, over and over again, lost in the wealth of emotion that had taken hold of them and refused to let go. Minutes later they were snuggled tightly together, their breaths syncing on each inhale and exhale, settling into each other's heartbeats until sleep sent them both to their dreams.

It was almost noon when Donovan woke from a deep slumber. He and Gianna had spent most of the night wide-awake, making love again and again. Their loving had been sweet and gentle, then Gianna had taken their intimate connection south, her ministrations dirty and hard. He'd lost count of the number of times she'd brought him to orgasm, each one like an out-of-body experience. The last time had been back in the shower just before they'd passed out in his bed, the morning sun beginning to peek through the window.

He stretched his body lengthwise and yawned as he rolled against the mattress. Reaching for Gianna, he found the bed empty. He jumped, startled to find her gone. The barest hint of disappointment billowed through his spirit. Rising, he moved into the bathroom. When his face was washed and his teeth polished to a bright white shine, he headed for his kitchen.

Gianna was seated at the kitchen table wearing one of his dress shirts. One knee was pulled to her chest, the other leg dangling casually off the wooden stool. She sat writing in her notepad, her attention focused on the words flying out of her pen. She was so absorbed in her work, she didn't notice him until he'd eased to her side and gently planted a warm kiss against her neck.

She purred softly. "Hmm! *Buon pomeriggio, come stai?*"

He kissed her again. "Good afternoon, and I would have been better if you had been in the bed when I woke. But thank you for asking."

She giggled as she tilted her head to kiss his lips. "Sorry about that, but I sometimes have to follow my muse when it leads me."

He nodded in understanding. "Something smells really good."

She nodded. "Signora Rossi left breakfast. There's fresh pastry in the oven, muesli and yogurt in the icebox, and I can pour you a cup of cappuccino whenever you're ready."

"I can do it," he said. "You keep writing."

"I actually think I'm done," she said as she laid down her pen. "I'll type up my notes when I get back home." She took a sip of the fresh coffee he'd poured for her.

Donovan moved from the counter to join her at the dining table. He came to an abrupt halt, spying an easel and oversize blank canvas sitting in the corner of the room. He pointed with his index finger. "What's that?"

She tossed a quick glance in the direction he pointed. "I thought you could paint," she answered, her own finger pointing to the supplies that rested on the coffee table. "I bought oils, watercolors, acrylics and a ton of brushes. There's also extra canvas, canvas board and some other stuff the man at the art store said you might like."

"Wow!" he exclaimed once, and then again. "Wow!"

She smiled. "You only live once and it's something you wanted to try, so I think now is as good a time as any."

He took a seat beside her, taking a moment to sip his coffee. "Before I forget again, how do you know Sophie Mugabe? I saw you two talking yesterday."

Gianna looked up to meet his curious gaze. "What makes you think I know her?"

"I saw you two talking yesterday," he repeated facetiously.

She rolled her eyes. "Last year we dated the same man. He was an English professor there at the university."

"At the same time?"

"Unfortunately. He wasn't honest about dating the two of us. We both found out when she showed up unannounced at his apartment and walked in on him and me unexpectedly."

Donovan eyed her with a raised brow. "I'm sure that was interesting!"

"There might have been some words exchanged and a punch or two thrown. It wasn't pretty, and definitely not one of my proudest moments."

His eyes widened. "Now that sounds like a Jerry Springer fiasco."

"Jerry who?"

"I guess I'm not the only one who needs to brush up on my pop culture." He laughed.

She narrowed her gaze on him.

"It's not important," he said, meeting her stare. "So what happened to the guy?"

"After they wired his jaw, he moved to Florence. At least that's what I was told."

"You broke his jaw?"

She tossed up her hands, a smile twitching at the edge of her mouth. "Why does everyone think that I had to be the one to break his jaw? Why couldn't she have broken his jaw?"

"Did Professor Mugabe break the man's jaw?"

"No. But that's not the point."

Donovan laughed. "So, that means you have a serious right hook. You are just full of surprises!"

"I reacted in the heat of the moment."

"And Sophie?"

"She's still holding a grudge like I purposely dated a man she was interested in."

He suddenly thought back to his last conversation with the woman.

"What?" Gianna asked, eyeing him curiously.

They locked gazes. "You might be," he said with a slight shrug.

Gianna stared for a brief moment, then shook her head, understanding washing over her expression. "So that's why she got so heated when I told her I was there to see you!"

"She got heated?"

"Royally! Why didn't you tell me you and she had something going on?" She leaned back in her seat and crossed her arms over her chest. "Because I do not play second to any other woman!"

Donovan laughed. "There's nothing going on between the two of us, and you are my one and only."

"But she likes you?"

"She does."

"And she wants to be in a relationship with you?"

He nodded. "But I told her that couldn't happen because I only see her as a friend and colleague, nothing more."

She hesitated for a split second. "Don't trust her. She's one of those women who puts the *fury* in 'hell hath no fury.'"

"I don't think…" he started, before being interrupted.

"David had a stellar reputation at the university. Granted, our little incident didn't bode well for him, but me breaking his jaw was the least of his problems. I made him hurt for breaking my heart, but she set out to destroy him. By the time she was done, he wasn't able to teach. At least not anywhere here in Italy."

"It couldn't have been that bad," he said, his tone hopeful.

Gianna shook her head. "It was worse than bad. Do not, I repeat, do not trust her."

The sound of rushing water suddenly bore down against the rooftop. The weatherman's prediction of bad weather with torrential rains had finally materialized. Donovan rose and moved to the front door, staring outside. Gianna eased her body against his, her thin arms wrapping around his waist as she looked past him.

"There goes my picnic lunch down by the beach," Donovan said.

"We were picnicking today?"

"I thought it would be a nice idea."

"We can picnic here instead. While you paint my portrait."

He nodded and smiled. "We can definitely do that."

She squeezed him, tightening her arms around his torso. "We can also go back to bed," she said as she released her grip and turned, moving back toward the bedroom. As she disappeared through the doorway, she tossed him a seductive wink over her shoulder as she let that dress shirt fall to the floor, her naked backside beckoning him to follow.

Chapter 11

As Donovan moved into the room, Gianna lay sprawled out on the bed, her naked body posed seductively atop the pillows. Moving to the foot of the bed, he stood staring down at her, marveling at just how beautiful she was.

Gianna lifted her torso upward, her weight resting on her elbows and forearms. A pointed toe slowly trailed the length of her other leg as she pulled her knee to her chest and pushed her leg down again. As he eyed her, lust searing in his gaze, her nipples hardened and she couldn't suppress the shiver that quickened her breath and raced the length of her spine. Her pulse rate soared.

Donovan lifted one knee and then the other, crawling onto the mattress top. He grabbed her foot and pulled her toward him, the gesture possessive and demanding as he straddled his body above hers.

Gianna reached up to wrap her arms around his neck, pulling him against her as she kissed his lips. This time there was nothing gentle about the connection, not like the many times before. It was rough and fiercely passionate as she thrust her tongue toward the back of his throat. She could barely stifle a moan as he drew her closer to deepen the embrace.

Lips and tongues were moving rapidly, both tasting like the strawberries and grapes they'd shared over breakfast. Donovan's kisses moved from her mouth down to her neck as he nibbled at the soft flesh, leaving a love bite against her skin. He lowered his head to slowly draw his tongue across one breast as he pinched the other lightly with his thumb and forefinger.

Gianna inhaled swiftly, the sharp intake of breath moving him to lift his eyes to her face. Rapture painted her expression, her eyes closed and her head thrown back against her neck. He resumed his salacious ministrations, his hands traveling slowly across her stomach and downward. The trek was teasing, fingers kneading and massaging until he was able to slip his large hand between her thighs, two fingers dipping into her sweet spot. She parted her legs to allow him easier access, and he dragged a fingernail across her slit and the pad of his thumb tapped at her clit, the pressure against her love button moving her to moan. He repeated the action again and again until Gianna was fighting to catch her breath, her moans like the sweetest balm.

He dipped his fingers deeper, penetrating her opening. The gesture met with copious fluid that made the transition seamless. He slowly thrust one finger and then three, furiously rubbing the sensitive spot until she was close to orgasm. He felt her tense, her muscles beginning to contract around his thrusting fingers. And then she cried out, tipping off the edge of ecstasy.

The two made love for hours, over and over again, the entire weekend lost in Donovan's bed. Donovan couldn't fathom any intimate connection being sweeter. He loved her intensely, every fiber in his being needing her. Wanting her like he'd never wanted anyone else. And when the sky darkened that last night, his manhood throbbing like a piston between her legs, Gianna whispered in his ear, the words *I love you* echoing around the room.

Franco stood at the kitchen stove, the ingredients for a tomato-based sauce resting atop the counters. When Gianna entered the home, he paused to stare as he reached for a dishcloth to swipe his hands clean.

"Buongiorno, papà," she chimed as she kissed his cheek, then took a seat at the counter.

Her father nodded. "Welcome home. I was starting to think that I was going to have to send the troops out to find you."

Gianna reached for a stalk of celery, pulling the vegetable to her lips. "Please, like we don't both know that Signora Rossi was keeping you posted on my whereabouts."

Her father laughed. "She may have told me something. She knows I'm a concerned father!"

"That's why she told you *everything*! I'll never understand why you two never married."

"We never married because I have only loved one woman in my life, and that was your mother. Felice Rossi is a sweet person and a good friend, but she could never hold a candle to my Angela." His gaze shifted as he fell into the memories of the woman who was gone. He changed the subject. "So, things are good with this young man of yours?"

She nodded. "Things are very good! Donovan's…" She paused, her eyes shifting from side to side. She suddenly looked back up at her father. "I love him, *papà*," she said, voicing aloud what had been in her heart for a while.

Her father smiled. "He's a good man. I like him, and I know he'll do right by you. I look forward to our becoming friends. And I'll be even happier when I can call him son. I will be able to call him son, right? And soon?"

Gianna laughed. "I don't know about that, *papà*! We'll have to see."

"Have you talked about it? About what you want out of the relationship?"

"We're still learning each other. I'm not trying to rush things."

"You spent the weekend with that man. I think you've already rushed things."

Color flushed Gianna's cheeks a deep shade of red. This time she was the one to change the subject. "Where are Carina and Graham?"

"They went to visit his parents. They'll be back at the end of the week."

Nodding, she rose from her seat. "If you need me

I'll be in my office. I have some work I need to catch up on."

Her father turned back to his sauce. "Let's walk the vineyards later. I want to see if the rain did any damage," he called after her. "And we can finish our conversation about your new boyfriend's intentions!"

Donovan couldn't remember ever being so happy. Waking next to Gianna had spoiled him, everything about their time together confirming what he wanted for his future. Their future together. When they hadn't been making love, they'd talked, some of the conversations mindless ramblings, others intense debates. And he'd painted, testing the waters for a retirement hobby. He'd approached the task with reservation until Gianna had pushed him to just let go and let whatever came to him be. The beginnings of a few projects had him excited to try again. And painting a trail of flowers across Gianna's butt had excited him.

Once or twice they'd simply fallen into the quiet, enjoying how the other breathed. It had been easy to be with her, and even when she had him dancing naked in the middle of his kitchen, a protruding erection bouncing in time to some dance tune, his comfort level had been at an all-time high. Gianna had a way of pushing him to let go and do things he would not necessarily do if left to his own devices. Her devil-may-care attitude had transcended his conservative one, and together they meshed nicely.

He hadn't wanted to take her home, and driving her back to the winery had been heartbreaking. They'd parted with a gentle kiss, Gianna promising to catch up with him the minute his day was through. Together they were electricity and fire, and with her gone he could feel the energy that filled him waiting to be re-ignited.

The hour-long ride to the school allowed him to pull himself together, to seriously think about the two of them and where they might be headed. Gianna made his heart sing, and he was past ready to fully commit to her and the relationship. The dynamics of how they'd come together and their brief bump in the road spoke to where they both were in their lives and where they wanted to be. Both had been searching for something that was missing, something neither had any idea they'd needed. Until they found each other. They complemented each other, as both had been whole to start with. It was the perfect icing on some very sweet cake!

Pulling into the school's parking lot and exiting his car, Donovan practically skipped to the front door. He anticipated having a very good day, the excitement gleaming in his eyes. He wasn't expecting Dr. Northway, the school's director, to meet him at the door.

"Dr. Northway, *buongiorno!*"

The man nodded, a quick snap of his neck and head. "Dr. Boudreaux, if you'll join me in my office, *per favore*." His tone was brusque, almost abrasive, his expression stone-cold. He turned abruptly and headed down the hallway, expecting Donovan to follow behind him.

As he did, Donovan suddenly got the distinct impression that his good mood was about to be shot to hell.

* * *

Gianna slammed her phone down against the desktop. She'd been trying to reach Donovan since lunchtime, and he hadn't returned any of her calls. She'd been half tempted to ride down to his cottage, but she didn't want to come across as that type of woman: obsessive, jealous and untrusting. Because she was none of those things, and never had been. And she didn't want to think he was that kind of man, done once he'd bedded her. Because she knew he was better than that, but he hadn't answered his phone or returned any of her calls since saying goodbye and wishing her a good day.

Her intuition told her something was amiss, and she was worried because she knew in her heart Donovan would have wanted to talk with her as much as she wanted to speak with him. Something or someone was keeping Donovan from at least sending her a text message. From whispering the words he'd whispered in her ear over the weekend. From wanting her to know how much he loved and desired her.

The weekend had been flawless. She'd given herself to him without hesitation, not an ounce of doubt about their commitment to each other. From day one, Donovan had said and done all the right things. He'd been sweet and caring, wooing her slowly. His actions had mirrored his words, and she'd known beyond any and all doubts that he was the one for her. Their relationship was sheer perfection!

Outside the air had cooled nicely, and the barest sliver of a moon hung in the dark sky. A gentle breeze blew through the open window behind her. Gianna jumped from her seat, feeling as if the winds had whispered to her. Something was wrong, and she had to figure out what it was. She would start at the cottage, she thought, and if he wasn't there, she would drive to the university and make someone there let her in to search for him.

Just as she reached for her coat and keys, there was a knock on her office door. Pulling it open, she was surprised to find her father standing on the other side.

"Where are you off to?" he questioned, his eyes dropping to the keys in her hand.

"I was going to go see Donovan. I haven't been able to reach him."

Her father nodded. "Probably because your young man has been in the vineyard talking with me."

"He's here?" Her eyes widened.

Franco nodded. "He's been here for a couple of hours now. I was outside when he drove up, and I could see something was on his mind, so I made him come help me check the vineyards. It gave me a chance to talk to him about his intentions."

Her eyes widened even more. "You didn't?"

Her father laughed. "I most certainly did. Now, I'm going to go grab a quick shower. Donovan is prepping the pasta. We should be ready to eat in about thirty minutes."

Gianna tossed her keys aside and dropped her coat to the floor. Her father was still laughing heartily as she pushed past him, headed for the kitchen.

Donovan stood at the counter chopping vegetables. His brow was furrowed in thought as he sliced and diced tomatoes picked from her father's gardens. Three large steaks were marinating in a glass dish, and a pot of water was just beginning to simmer for the fettuccine.

Gianna paused in the doorway, staring. He wore her father's apron, the one given to him by her mother. In all her years, she'd never known her father to let anyone else wear the treasured garment. Clearly, she thought, Donovan had made quite an impression.

"*Ciao*, Donovan," she said as she entered the room. She moved to his side to kiss his cheek.

Donovan turned to meet her lips instead, his mouth dancing easily over hers. *"Ciao, bella!"*

"I was worried about you."

"I'm sorry. I would have called you back, but your father..."

She held up a hand, stalling the rest of his comment. "Say no more. I know my father," she said with a smile.

Her eyes flitted over his face, and she could see the stress that tensed the muscles. "What's wrong?"

Donovan shook his head, fighting to pull a smile onto his face. "Let's talk about it later," he said, turning to toss minced garlic and onion in the pan with the tomatoes.

"Let's talk about it now," she said as she eased to his other side, clasping her hand over his.

He met the look she gave him as he relinquished the spoon, leaving her to stir his sauce. He took a deep inhale before answering. "Dr. Northway met me at the door this morning and called me to his office."

"The school's director?"

He nodded. "A female student has filed a formal complaint against me for inappropriate conduct. She

claims I asked for a sexual favor in exchange for giving her a passing grade. She says that when she told me
no, I threatened to fail her. I was given the choice to
hand in my resignation and leave the school quietly or
to appear before a disciplinary review committee next
week and risk being terminated and having my work
visa pulled permanently."

"And you told him you were going to fight the allegations, correct?"

He nodded. "I did. Either way, though, just the hint
of any kind of impropriety could kill my career."

"You do know that this is all Sophie Mugabe's doing.
I warned you!"

"I know that she supposedly received the complaint
and passed it on to the administration. So she's had a
hand in it somehow."

"We're not going to let her get away with this."

Donovan sighed and kissed Gianna one more time.
"I want you to know that I didn't do this," he said.

"I know that."

"Your father wasn't so sure. He asked a lot of questions."

"He just does that. It's a father thing. He was sure."

"How do you know?"

She tapped the gray cotton fabric embroidered with
the word *Chef* across the front. Donovan looked confused.

"My mother gave him this. He's never let anyone
wear it. He was sure." She looped her arms around his
neck and hugged him tightly.

Tears misted Donovan's eyes as he hugged her back.

When he'd come to the winery, wanting Gianna to re-assure him that everything was going to be all right, he hadn't given any thought to what he would say to her father. Franco had been in the front yard when he'd pulled in, and when the patriarch had commanded Don-ovan to join him in the vineyards, he'd gone reluctantly.

For the first half hour all they'd talked about were grapes and the best grapes for the best wines. Then the old man had asked him what was wrong, and Dono-van was suddenly giving him a detailed blow-by-blow recap of his meeting with the school's administrator and being temporarily removed from his teaching position. Franco had listened intently, allowing Donovan to spill until he didn't have anything else to say.

"So, did you do it?" the old man had asked him.

Donovan had shaken his head steadfastly. "No, sir. I didn't. I'm not that kind of man."

"Why would this young woman say such a thing?"

"I honestly don't know. I did reject her advances, so I think she's trying to get revenge. But I would never compromise my integrity like that. And I would *never* disrespect Gianna like that."

Franco had nodded, then just like that, he'd changed the subject. "Has my daughter talked to you about her mother at all?"

He'd shaken his head. "No, sir. She always changes the subject when I bring her up."

Franco gestured for him to take a seat, and the two rested on one of the wooden benches in the garden. Gi-anna's father leaned forward, resting his arms against his thighs as he thought about the history that would soon be the story he would tell. Minutes passed before he finally cleared his throat and spoke.

"Gianna was devastated when her mother died. Both girls were, but it hit Gianna harder. She and my Angela were together when that blood vessel burst in Angela's head. Gianna had gotten into trouble with Sister Mary Frances at the school. Gianna was always smarter than the average bear, and she had no problems making sure you knew it. She was bored in class and smart-mouthed the nun, and they called her mother. Angela and I had already decided that Gianna needed to be moved up a grade, and so Angela went down to the school to talk to them about doing that. They were waiting for Carina to get out of class, and then my girls were all going to go get gelato. She and her mother were sitting together, and then Angela just slumped over and was gone. For years, Gianna blamed herself. She thought that if she had just been a good girl, then Angela wouldn't have been stressed. And if she hadn't been stressed, she wouldn't have had the aneurysm. I sometimes think she still blames herself."

The man swiped a tear from his eye as he continued his story. "Angela was an exchange student doing a semester at the university when we met. I was much older and already running the winery. Mutual friends introduced us, and I thought she was the most beautiful vision I'd ever laid eyes on. Everything about her was warm. Warm brown eyes, warm brown skin and the warmest, sweetest spirit of any woman I'd ever known. My girls are just like their mother!

"Angela had a roommate at the university. A girl

named Gina Puccini. Gina's father was a government official in Nice. Gina had a crush on me, and she wasn't happy about me liking Angela. She wasn't very nice to Angela when she found out we were seeing each other. She tried everything she could think of to break us up. She lied and said that Angela was seeing other boys at the school. Wouldn't give her my messages. Would show up at group events and try to monopolize my attention. She made things very difficult for the two of us." Franco sighed heavily as the memories flooded his spirit. He paused briefly before continuing.

"One day I had planned to take Angela to dinner, and I went to pick her up. I arrived early because she hadn't gotten back from class yet, but Gina was there in the room. We exchanged words, and I told her I would never love anyone the way I loved Angela. She stormed out, and I thought it was over. Minutes later the police were there asking me questions. Gina was down the hall crying, her clothes torn, claiming that I had assaulted her. When Angela arrived, they were taking me away in handcuffs.

"Angela saved my life and my business. Had I been convicted, it would have been all over. But she did everything she could to discredit Gina's story. And Angela went up against Gina's father, who was determined to see me pay for what his daughter said I did. It was not a good time.

"Gina finally admitted that she lied, but the stigma of people thinking I might be a rapist followed me for a good long while. Some even said that my Angela couldn't do better than a man like me because she was a black woman, and only a rapist would want a woman like her. But Angela never let any of that keep us from loving each other and our girls."

"I'm so sorry that you two had to go through that."

Franco chuckled. "Me, too! And in all of our years together, my Angela never once asked me if I had done it. Her faith in me was unwavering. She loved me that much."

Donovan nodded, reflecting on the man's words.

"My Gianna, she loves you that much, Mr. Boudreaux," Franco added matter-of-factly.

Donovan shifted his eyes toward the man, the two locking gazes.

"I expect we'll be having a wedding soon, no? I won't have my daughter's good reputation sullied. These old bats in the village would love to talk badly about her."

Donovan nodded, a smile pulling at his full lips. "Yes, sir. I hope so."

"Soon, before the Carusos' daughter comes sniffing around for a husband!"

Donovan laughed. "No worries there, sir! I will never love anyone like I love my Gianna," he said.

Franco nodded his approval. "We should prepare dinner. I've worked up an appetite. Do you cook?"

As Donovan thought back to his time with his future father-in-law, he hugged Gianna close, grateful that she and her family had come into his life. Together, they were a formidable force to be reckoned with. Every ounce of worry suddenly subsided, dissipating like water on a hot pan.

Franco pulled the duo from their reverie. Moving into the room, he smiled as he eyed them wrapped comfortably around each other. He cleared his throat. "If burning the gravy is how you prove to me you can cook, you're doing a mighty fine job, son! A mighty fine job!"

Chapter 12

Gianna woke with a start, something dark chasing her in her dreams. Relief came the instant she opened her eyes and spied Donovan slumbering sweetly beside her. She eased her leg from under his and lifted herself up against the headboard to stare down at him.

He lay on his back with his legs splayed open, one hand cupping his privates. His head was rolled to the side, his face pressed between two pillows. He snored softly, the exhale ending in a low whistle. Watching him made Gianna smile.

After dining with her father, she'd followed Donovan back to his home. They'd been there ever since, only leaving once to meet with Gianna's attorney. Despite his reluctance, she'd insisted he needed legal representation. He'd argued the point, insisting that he hadn't done anything wrong. But as her lawyer had pointed out, it would come down to being his word against Alessandra's if they couldn't find any proof to refute the girl's claims.

Signora Rossi had fed them quite a few times, her maternal instincts kicking into full swing. She'd been fawning over them both, always squeezing his cheeks, and then hers, as the moment moved her. The older woman still fussed, giving Gianna a hard time, and she wouldn't have had it any other way. As she thought about them, Gianna admitted that one of her most favorite moments was Donovan and Signora Rossi practicing Italian and English together. He was learning quickly—their elderly friend not so much.

Donovan shifted his body, turning his back to her. He seemed to settle down, his breathing easy, and then he rolled back again, his arms outstretched as he reached for her. Once his hands touched her skin, his fingers warm against her thighs, he curled himself close against her. The nearness of him made Gianna smile.

He suddenly lifted his head to stare at her, his eyes thin slits as he struggled to focus. "Are you okay?" he mumbled.

She nodded, her voice a low whisper as she snuggled back down against him, wiggling her butt against his crotch. "I'm fine, *amore mio*. Go back to sleep."

And he did, closing his eyes and drifting back into his dreams.

Gianna had only been asleep for a few hours when Donovan's hands trailing across her body pulled her from her rest. His fingertips glided across her stomach to her breasts and back, dipping low to gently pull at the swirls of hair between her legs. His touch tickled, and she could feel herself smiling in her sleep.

His warm breath blew gently against the back of her neck, and a full, hammer-hard erection pressed like steel against her butt. She felt him moving slowly against her, a gentle back-and-forth gyration as he used her body to massage himself.

Donovan whispered, "Are you asleep?"

Gianna chuckled softly. "How can I sleep with you teasing me like that?" she purred.

"Sorry," he apologized. "This woke me up." He rotated his hips against her a second time, the bulge between his legs like steel.

Gianna giggled softly. "That feels like it might be a problem. I think we should do something about it," she whispered in reply.

He nodded, his head bobbing against a pile of pillows. "I think so."

Gianna suddenly pulled her body from his, spinning around to face him. His eyes opened wider as she began to kiss her way down the length of his torso, pressing her mouth to that spot beneath his chin, his broad chest and the well of his belly button, until she'd crawled down low beneath the sheets.

His erection stretched full and wide with desire. He was nicely endowed, and as she took him into the palm of her hand, his organ twitched with anticipation. Donovan sucked in a large gulp of air and held it, every muscle in his body clenched tightly.

Without hesitating, Gianna stuck out her tongue and

lightly licked the tip of his member. His whole body jumped, nerve endings firing rapidly. He blew out the breath he'd been holding and gasped out loud, his voice ringing through the early-morning air.

Gianna swirled her tongue over the head, then licked up and down his shaft, even tonguing his testicles. Donovan groaned with pure, unadulterated pleasure, her touch taking him right to the edge of ecstasy.

She sucked him in as she fisted the base, her hand and mouth moving in perfect sync. It was more than Donovan had anticipated, and he could feel himself giving in to the sensations that were sweeping through his body.

He moaned as he stroked the top of her head, his fingers tangling in the thick curls. "So…so…good!" he stammered, the words coming with a raspy breath. He started to move his hips faster and faster, pushing himself in and out of her mouth. She clutched his butt with both hands to control his ministrations, her own body becoming heated, moisture pooling in her private crevices. She squeezed and manipulated the taut flesh, bringing him close to orgasm then pulling back until he couldn't hold on. With one final shove past her lips, Donovan exploded in her mouth, wave after wave of pleasure surging with a vengeance. "Oh, sweet Jesus!" he cried. *"Mio Dio!"*

Gianna savored the taste of him. She continued to suck and lick his organ as his body spasmed over and over again. When she finally pulled him from her mouth, she tilted her head back and swallowed.

Donovan was completely spent, his entire being feeling as if he'd gone through ten rounds. He pulled her into his arms and nuzzled his face into her neck. He could feel the hands of slumber beginning to pull him back into its clutches. Unable to fight it, he whispered her name, promising to return the gesture before the new day was done.

Carina burst into Gianna's office, storming through the door like a hurricane on steroids. Eyes wide, Gianna looked up from the chapter she was trying to finish, surprised to see her twin.

"What's wrong?" Gianna asked, a quiver of nervous energy like a shock wave through her system.

Carina dropped into the upholstered seat in front of her sister's desk. "What are we going to do about Donovan?"

"Excuse me?"

"Donovan. What are we going to do?"

"What are you talking about, Sissy?" Gianna leaned forward in her seat.

"Everyone is talking about Donovan and some girl from the school. They're saying she claims that he tried to take advantage of her and that he threatened her. It's all kinds of messy!"

Gianna blew a low sigh. "I know. He's hired Dante to represent him."

"Your attorney, Dante?"

She nodded. "Donovan has to defend himself before a university review board next week. There was no way I was going to let him do that on his own. His Italian's not that good yet!"

Carina nodded, blowing out a sigh of relief. "Dante's good. That's good! But what are *we* going to do? Because we can't let this girl get away with telling these lies."

Gianna smiled. "So you do believe him? You know he didn't do it?"

Her sister's expression was incredulous. "Of course I know he didn't do it! That is definitely not the kind of man I would fix you up with."

Gianna moved around the desk to give her sister a hug. The two held tight to each other, tears misting in both their eyes.

Carina shook herself free from the embrace. "You still haven't answered my question."

Gianna shrugged. "I don't know. It's been driving me crazy trying to figure out what's going on and how I can fix it. I do know that Mugabe woman is behind it, though."

Carina's gaze narrowed. "That professor who was dating your ex-boyfriend? Or were you dating her boyfriend?" She giggled. "You're referring to that third leg in that little ménage à trois of yours last year?"

She nodded. "One and the same. She's interested in Donovan and he rejected her. I know she's going after him to get even with him, and me."

"Then we're definitely about to burst her bubble!"

There was a pause as Gianna stood staring at her sister. Her smile slid slowly across her face. "What do you have in mind, Sissy?"

Carina grinned. "I think we need to take a ride."

* * *

Donovan sighed deeply into his cell phone receiver. On the other end, his mother was talking a mile a minute, voicing her disapproval and unhappiness in one big breath. He'd given up trying to ease her concerns, figuring once she got it out of her system they'd be able to move on. But it was starting to look as if she wasn't going to get over it anytime soon.

"I knew you going to Italy wasn't going to be a good idea."

"Mom, this has nothing to do with me being here in Italy. You know how these young people are today. They have an air of entitlement, no sense of responsibility and they don't concern themselves with how their bad behavior will impact other people. Unfortunately, this young woman is just plain messy. She's told a bold-faced lie, and now I have to deal with the consequences. But you and I both know the truth will always prevail."

"Well, I'm coming," Katherine said. "As soon as your father and I can get a flight out, we'll be there."

Donovan could hear his father fussing in the background.

"We don't need to go to Italy! That boy is grown. He knows how to handle his own business, Katherine!"

"I'm not talking to you, Senior Boudreaux!" Katherine fussed back. "I just know we're not going to let our baby go through this mess by himself. Now call Mason and see how soon we can get on one of his planes, please! And then call Katrina and have her recommend a good attorney over there."

Donovan chuckled, shaking his head. "Mom, please, you don't need to worry. We've got this handled."

"Donovan James Boudreaux, don't you tell me not to worry! I'm the parent in this relationship. It's my job to worry!"

He let out a gust of air past his full lips. "Yes, ma'am."

"Besides, it'll give me a chance to meet this young lady you've been seeing. Your brothers have told me a lot about her."

"You're really going to like her. Gianna's wonderful, Mom!"

"You haven't known her that long. You don't know what she is," his mother said matter-of-factly.

"I know her, Mom, and I love her," he said softly. "And you need to trust me on this."

There was a lengthy pause, and Donovan could visualize the expression across his mother's face: her gaze narrowed, her lips pursed and her jaw tight. He waited for the sharp comment that would remind him once again of his place as the child in their relationship. He knew that he and his siblings could be eighty years old, and their parents would still be reminding them of the respect that was their due.

He took a deep breath. "I promise, Mom, you won't be disappointed," he concluded.

Katherine sniffled, then cleared her throat. "You have never been a disappointment. Your father and I have always been proud of you. We love you, son."

Donovan smiled. "Thank you," he said. "And I love you both, too."

"Senior's on the phone with Mason now. He'll send you our flight information as soon as we know."

Donovan chuckled. "I guess that means I didn't change your mind, huh?"

His mother laughed with him. "I don't know why you even wasted your time trying!"

Gianna was seated in the student quad waiting for her sister to return. Around her, college kids were enjoying the afternoon weather, lounging on the grass and benches as they discussed courses, the opposite sex, music and a host of topics that had their voices ringing with laughter through the air.

She still didn't have a clue what Carina had up her sleeve, but she knew enough about her sister to be just a teensy bit concerned. She'd lost count of all the stunts her twin would pull that had gotten them both in trouble over the years.

She caught sight of her out of the corner of her eye, her look-alike moving in her direction. She carried a tray of food and was walking with two young women Gianna didn't recognize. She stared as they approached, Carina giggling with them as if she was in her teens again. Gianna smiled brightly as the trio joined her at the picnic table where she sat.

"Ciao!" she said brightly, nodding slightly.

"Hello!" one of the other women responded as she helped Carina with the food.

Carina pointed as she took a seat beside her sister. "This is Alessandra and Simona. They are both math

majors here at the university. And this is my sister, Gianna. She's a literature major."

Alessandra glanced from one to the other. "You two
look like twins!" she exclaimed.

Carina laughed. "Everybody says that, but she is
older than I am."

Gianna threw Carina a look, ignoring the smirk on
her sibling's face. "I'm not that much older," she said
with a giggle.

Alessandra nodded. "You should not cut your hair,"
she said to Carina before shifting her gaze to Gianna.
"I love your long curls!"

Gianna smiled. "I wish it was straight like yours.
Your hair is beautiful!"

Alessandra tossed her blond locks over one shoulder
and then the other, smiling brightly.

Simona eyed her warily. "You actually look familiar. Where do I know you from?"

Gianna shrugged. "Maybe we had a class together?"

"Or maybe you saw her on the back of a book," Carina said facetiously. "She has that kind of face." She
pursed her own lips and winked. "So do I, now that
you mention it!"

Alessandra giggled. "Simona's not big on reading.
I'm sure it couldn't have been a book!"

Gianna laughed, joining in the giggles.

Carina passed her sister a sandwich and a canned
soda. "Alessandra says these are the best, so I had to
try them," she said as she took a bite of her own sandwich, a meatball wedge laden with cheese. She nodded.
"Oh, they are really good!"

Alessandra's head bobbed. "Not as good as the ones you can get in Grosseto, but very close! Grosseto has the best meatballs, I think."

The four women sat enjoying their meal, the conversation casual as Carina made nice with her new best friends. Gianna marveled at how easily her sister manipulated the truth, the other two women actually believing they, too, were students. She was giggling over the boys and making plans to join them on a weekend trip to Rome. Anyone else would have thought they'd been best friends since forever, instead of new acquaintances chatting for the very first time.

Gianna was less inclined to be so nice. Despite Carina's efforts to pull her into the conversation, wanting her to play pretend right along with her, all Gianna wanted was to smack the smug look off Alessandra's face. The moment Carina had said she was a math major, Gianna had known who she was. Knowing the allegations the young woman had made against Donovan, the lies she had told, had Gianna seeing red, and it was difficult not to just punch the girl in her mouth. Her eyes skated back and forth between Alessandra and Simona as she forced her lips into a smile.

Carina swiped a paper napkin across her mouth. She locked eyes with her sister, her brows lifted. "I was telling them before about your problem with your professor. How he led you on, and then you found out he was married."

Simona shook her head from side to side. *"Gli uomini sono tutti i cani!"* she muttered.

Carina laughed. "Yes, men are all dogs!" she said in agreement.

Gianna tried not to let her emotions show on her face. "He broke my heart," she muttered, feigning heartbreak.

"So what happened?" Alessandra asked. She shifted forward in her seat, resting her elbows against the table and her head in her hands.

Gianna took a deep breath. "We were dating for months. We traveled together, and it was perfect. Then one day I was at his apartment, and we were making love when I hear the bedroom door open and this woman is suddenly screaming at us!"

Simona slapped a hand over her mouth. "She walked in on you?"

Gianna nodded. "We were naked in his bed. It was horrible!" she exclaimed, her tone exaggerated.

Carina laughed. "He was bottom up and head down. I'm sure it was quite a sight!"

The other two women laughed heartily.

Gianna cut a look at her sister. Amusement danced in Carina's eyes. "It wasn't pretty," she said.

Simona nodded. "You should do like Alessandra. She always gets even."

"You waste too much time holding a grudge. Get even and move on. That's my motto," Alessandra noted.

"Alessandra had a boyfriend who cheated. She got him drunk, set him up with the police chief's daughter, then posted pictures of the two online. The police chief ran him out of town!"

"You really did that?" Carina exclaimed. "You are my new hero!"

Alessandra shrugged, a devious smirk across her face. "Sometimes you just have to teach a man a lesson."

Simona nodded in agreement.

"I need to be more like you." Gianna laughed.

"I'm always available for hire," Alessandra said smugly.

Carina laughed. "Do you come with references?"

"As a matter of fact, I do," the girl said. "I'm helping out someone now. One of my professors."

Gianna glanced at her sister. "Do tell!" she said, both women shifting to the edge of their seats.

Chapter 13

The two women sat in their car after waving their good-byes to Simona and Alessandra. When the other car pulled out of sight, Gianna tossed up her hands in frustration.

"Aargh!" she screamed, tight fists clenched in front of her. "Do you believe her? She was actually bragging about what she was doing!"

Carina nodded, a wide smile across her face. "Yes, she was and it's a good thing, too!"

Gianna eyed her sister, confusion furrowing her brow. "Why is that a good thing?"

"How else was I going to get it on tape?" she said, holding up a small audio recorder. She pushed the re-wind button and then pushed Play. Alessandra's voice vibrated through the space. "He'll think twice about telling me no again!" She pushed the stop button.

"You taped it all?" Gianna asked, her eyes widening.

Her sister grinned. "Everything we needed."

Gianna threw her arms around her sister's neck and hugged her tightly. Tears suddenly streamed down her face, a weight feeling as if it had been lifted off her shoulders. Carina hugged her back, swiping at the moisture that had pooled behind her own eyelids.

"We're not done yet," Carina said as she pushed Gianna away.

"What do you mean? We have her on tape."

"We do, but we have to get that Mugabe woman, too. Luckily for us, Alessandra said they were meeting at the Duomo tonight. She invited us to go along."

"How are we going to do that? Sophie Mugabe knows me! And even with your short hair, we still look alike. She'll know who you are the minute she lays eyes on you."

Carina nodded. "Which is why we're not able to go," she said as she dialed a number on her cell phone and waited for it to ring.

Curiosity shifted in Gianna's eyes as she sat waiting for her sister to complete her call. Her smile returned when the party answered on the other end.

"Graham, honey, it's me! I need you to go to Florence. Gianna and I really need your help!"

The three most important men in the Martelli women's lives sat staring at the duo, completely floored by the story they told. Franco shook his head from side to side, his arms crossed evenly over his chest. Graham sat at the counter, nothing about what he'd participated in surprising him. Donovan was the only one who was visibly stunned by what had transpired. He looked from one woman to the other, then shot a glance toward Graham and the family patriarch.

They had played the audio tapes twice, the first recording of Alessandra and the second of Alessandra and Sophie Mugabe. Both conversations left no doubt of Donovan's innocence and the twisted plot between the two women. He still didn't understand how the twins had managed to pull it off.

"So you actually befriended Alessandra?" he asked.

Gianna shook her head. "Not me. Carina. That witch was lucky I didn't smack the mess out of her because I really wanted to hit her." Disdain painted her expression.

Carina laughed. "You will never win any awards for your acting."

"I'm still confused," Donovan said.

Carina leaned across the counter. "Alessandra is narcissistic, and she craves attention. I followed her on Instagram and started commenting on her photos. When we went to the school, I pretended we'd just run into each other, and when I commented on her social media account and flattered her vanity, she couldn't wait to be my friend," Carina said with a shrug. "It was Psychology 101, and she fell for it. We just got lucky with the rest of it."

"Very lucky," Graham interjected, "and it's a good thing, too, because Carina was ready to break into her apartment and commit too many crimes to mention. At least all I had to do was sit at the table next to them, turn on the recorder and sip my drink."

"And you actually got that close that you were able to record them in the club?" Donovan questioned.

Graham nodded. "I even danced with the blonde! My wife gave me very specific orders!"

"I just want to know how they finagled you into their scheme," Franco stated.

Graham shrugged, his broad shoulders pushing toward the ceiling. "You know I can't say no to your daughter! She scares me!"

The older man laughed. "*Figlio*, you better learn before she gets you locked up behind bars one day!"

Both Donovan and Gianna had been excited to turn over copies of the audio tapes to Dante the attorney. After hearing how they'd acquired them and listening to the transmissions, he assured Donovan that he had nothing to be concerned about. *"Risolveremo il piu rapidamente possibile,"* Dante had said, promising to resolve the matter promptly. It was now just a matter of time before they'd know the outcome.

The drive back to Maremma was quiet, the two enjoying the quiet and the low melody of the music playing on the car radio. The weather was near perfect—the temperature ideal, the sky a brilliant shade of blue and a bright sun shining above the treetops.

As Donovan rode shotgun, he was awed by the sheer beauty of the landscape. Minutes passed before he turned to stare at Gianna, reaching a large palm out to caress her thigh. The ease of his touch made her smile.

She shifted her gaze in his direction, her eyes wafting back and forth between him and the road. "Are you happy, Donovan?" she asked as he trailed his fingers against her profile.

He smiled "Very. Are you?"

She nodded. "You make me happy!"

"Gianna, have you ever thought about living in the United States?"

She turned her gaze on him and held it for a split second. Donovan felt the vehicle slow down significantly before she refocused her gaze.

She shook her head. "No, I haven't," she answered honestly.

"Do you think you can ever leave Tuscany?"

She answered his question with a question of her own. "Would you consider staying?"

Donovan smiled. "We really need to decide what we're going to do. I want to make an honest woman of you, and that needs to happen before your father and my mother join forces."

She laughed. "Define honest."

He smiled. "I'm hoping you'll be the next Mrs. Donovan Boudreaux."

"The next? Was there a last Mrs. Boudreaux?"

His expression was smug. "No, but you never know. There might be another in the future."

Gianna scoffed. "Not if I have anything to say about it!"

They giggled together softly.

"So, what do you want to do?" she asked.

He paused in thought before answering. "I know for certain that I can get work in the United States. I'm not so sure what's going to happen here. Not that I'm worried about supporting us because we can live quite comfortably off my savings and investments if I never teach another day in my life. But I don't want to stop teaching."

Gianna nodded but said nothing, seeming to fall into thought. It was a good few minutes before she spoke again.

"This is my home. It's all I've ever known. I never imagined not being able to work the vineyards or help my father with the winery. But..." She hesitated a second time.

Donovan prodded. "But?"

She took a deep breath. "But... I will follow you wherever you want to go. I trust that you will always do what will be in the best interest of our family. So...if we need to live in America, that's where we will live. I can write anywhere."

He kissed her cheek. "I love you, Gianna Martelli. I love you with everything in me!"

Her smile was engaging, emotion misting her bright eyes. "I love you, too, *mio caro*. I love you, too!"

"I want babies with you, Gianna. Five or six."

Gianna laughed. "Now you've lost your mind! One set of twins and we're done."

"You say that now, but I can be quite persuasive. And we might not get twins the first few times, so we'll have to keep trying," he teased.

She pulled the car into the parking area outside the

winery. Stepping out of the vehicle, she stood still, her gaze roaming the countryside. She suddenly couldn't see herself ever leaving the Tuscan heat, a wave of melancholy washing over her. And then she turned to stare at Donovan, the beauty of his smile assuring her that everything would be well no matter where they settled in the world, taking that Tuscan heat with them.

Reading her mind, Donovan moved to her side, easing his body against hers. With her back pressed against his chest and his arms wrapped around her waist, he pressed his face into her lush curls and kissed the top of her head. The scent of her perfume teased his nostrils.

In the distance, the sun was just beginning its descent, the wealth of it falling behind the trees in the distance. The sky blazed in shades of red, yellow and purple, a kaleidoscope of colors that made the view look like a priceless work of art.

"We have the most beautiful sunsets here in Maremma," she whispered.

Donovan nodded in agreement as he tightened the hold he had her wrapped in. He spun her around in his arms, his stare meeting hers. "You'll never miss one," he said. "This is our home, and here is where I want to see our children raised."

Gianna's eyes widened. "*Sei sicuro,* Donovan?"

"I am very sure. You have to be happy or I won't be."

She threw her arms around him, and the tears she'd been fighting spilled over her cheeks.

The late night ride atop the two horses was a perfect ending to the day. Gianna rode Raffaello and Donovan had saddled Michelangelo, a large black Arabian stallion with a majestic gait and a coat that was pitch-black in color.

There was a full moon in the dark sky, seeming almost like a spotlight leading their way. It was a slow stroll down to the coastal way as they rode side by side, trading easy conversation. Once on the damp sand, Gianna lowered her reins and applied pressure with her knees to transition Raffaello to a slow trot. Donovan and Michelangelo followed behind them.

Once they reached Gianna's secret cove they dismounted, the horses moving to stand in the only grassy area high up on a hill. Hand in hand, the couple walked the shoreline, savoring the cool evening air that wafted off the water.

Coming to a stop, Gianna turned into him, sliding easily into Donovan's arms. She reached up to kiss his mouth. He wrapped her in his arms and held her as he tossed a look over his shoulder and up the beach.

"I want to make love to you," he whispered loudly. "Right here, right now."

She laughed. "Then you should."

"Someone might see us."

She laughed again. "Don't let that stop you."

Fervor danced in Donovan's eyes. He watched as Gianna took a step back, slipping the T-shirt she wore over her head, exposing her bare breasts. He threw a look over his shoulder a second time, then wiped away the sweat that had beaded across his brow with the back of his hand. As Gianna pushed her sweatpants down to the sand beneath her feet, he tore at his own clothes until they were both naked.

With a wink and a giggle, Gianna skipped to the shoreline and then into the warm water.

"Are you coming?" she called out, laughter spilling past her lips.

Nervous energy sent a shiver up Donovan's spine. Without giving it a second thought, he raced behind her.

They swam and danced in the warm waters. Kissed beneath the star-filled sky. The moon caressed and teased them as they made the sweetest love, their bodies carving imprints in the damp sand. Donovan loved her easily, oblivious to their surroundings. In that moment he felt immensely blessed. The intimacy between them was a mélange of everything that was good and decent, those things they loved most, wrapped in the prettiest paper and tied with one big bow. Perfection defined the love the two felt for each other, and in that moment, beneath that full moon, life was the best it had ever been.

The call came four days later, Dr. Northway apologizing profusely and asking Donovan to report immediately back to the classroom.

"Miss Donati has been suspended for the rest of the semester, and after some discussion, Professor Mugabe felt it was in everyone's best interest that she resign. And once you're settled back in, we'd like to talk to you about possibly assuming the department chair position."

Donovan nodded into the receiver. "I'll have to think about it," he answered. "For now, I think it's important that I fulfill my contractual obligation and finish out the school year. We can talk more on Monday when I return."

Dr. Northway had apologized one last time before hanging up the phone. Donovan pumped his fist in the air, a huge grin filling his face. He'd been expecting the director's call. Dante had called earlier that morning to give him the news that he'd been completely vindicated. Donovan was grateful, but he still found himself feeling some kind of way and didn't have the words to explain it. Before the call he'd been painting, his easel and chair sitting out on the patio as he stared out to the vast green fields. Signora Rossi had fussed about earlier, leaving them a pretty salad, an antipasto tray and two ramekins of panna cotta.

Gianna looked up from the story she was working on, five hundred pages of copyedits she needed to complete and return to her editor. "Are you okay?" she asked, concern wafting between them.

"I don't know. I'm happy that it's over but I don't know if I want to go back."

"But you want to teach, right?"

He nodded. "There's nothing else I'd rather be doing. But I don't know if this position is the right one."

"Well, the secondary school is always an option if you like teenagers."

Donovan contemplated the comment for a brief moment. "I might give that some thought," he said, moving back toward the door.

She smiled. "How's the painting coming along?"

He grinned. "I think I'm about to give Picasso a run for his money!"

"Picasso?" She laughed. "That should be interesting."

"Extremely!"

Before Donovan could get out the door, his cell phone chimed against the countertop. He moved back inside to answer the call.

"It's my brother," he said as he engaged the device. "Hey, Kendrick! I have you on speaker. Say hi to Gianna!"

"Hey, there! Hi, Gianna! How are you?"

"I'm good, Kendrick. How are you?"

"I just called to warn you two. We all just landed."

"We all who?" Donovan asked as he and Gianna exchanged a look.

His brother laughed. "Everybody! The whole family is here!"

Chapter 14

Donovan's family came in like a storm wind. They were loud and forward, and in a split second after their arrival he remembered what it was about all of them that he missed most.

Even Tarah, with all her annoying ways, brought a smile to his face. "Don Juan finally has a girlfriend!" she exclaimed as she gave Gianna a warm hug.

Gianna laughed. "Don Juan?"

"Our nickname for him because he was always such a ladies' man...*not!*"

Donovan rolled his eyes. His mother still had an arm around his waist, hugging him warmly.

"Leave your brother alone, Tarah. Go outside and explore! There's a reason we left all the kids back in the States!"

Tarah rolled her eyes, pushing her lips into a feigned pout.

"Where are the kids?" Donovan asked, inquiring about his nephews and nieces.

Katrina grabbed Matthew's hand. "This is an adults-only excursion. We left all the babies in Dallas with Matthew's family."

Katherine laughed. "My grandbabies are all being spoiled rotten! You know how them Stallions do!" She gave Donovan another squeeze as she changed the subject. "I'm so glad you were able to resolve that mess with the university. But we were all prepared to be right here by your side at that hearing."

Donovan nodded. "Thank you, but now you all can just enjoy your time here."

"How long are you all staying?" Gianna asked.

"Not too long," Mason answered.

"Long enough for some of us to get into trouble, I'm sure." Maitlyn giggled. She wrapped a protective arm around her pregnant belly.

"Won't be none of that," Senior interjected. "I'm not bailing anyone out!"

"I just want to know where the boys are!" Tarah quipped.

Their mother pointed her index finger. "Outside!" she said, her eyebrows raised at her youngest child.

The chatter continued as the family inspected Donovan's small space, his artwork and the landscape outside, and interrogated Gianna.

"This is absolutely delightful!" Katherine exclaimed.

"It's small," Senior said. "And there's nothing wrong with small."

Donovan shook his head. "I wasn't expecting a family reunion anytime soon," he said.

Donovan's brother Guy laughed. "You people are going to scare Donovan's new friend away."

Gianna gave Donovan a look, her smile bright. "I'm not going anywhere," she said.

"How did you two meet?" Tarah asked. "I mean, Don Juan here hasn't been in Italy long enough to suddenly have a girlfriend."

The couple traded a look as the room quieted, everyone waiting for a response.

"We met online," Donovan said.

"My sister introduced us," Gianna said at the same time.

Confusion washed over everyone's expression. Shaking his head, Donovan told them their story from the beginning, Gianna filling in any details he missed. When they were done, there was silence, everyone exchanging amused looks.

Tarah suddenly burst out laughing. "Only you, Don Juan! Only you could make dating a textbook topic for what to do and how not to do it!"

The laughter was abundant, and it filled the space with an immense amount of joy. In the kitchen, his mother and Signora Rossi were in deep conversation. The family members marveled at how easily the two women seemed to intuitively know what the other was saying, although one was speaking English and the other Italian. Together, the antipasto and salad Signora Rossi had prepared earlier was enough for the Boudreaux army to all snack on. At one point the duo burst into laughter and Gianna blushed profusely, shaking her head.

"What?" Donovan asked, wrapping his arms around the woman.

Gianna laughed. "You really don't want to know!" she said as she moved back to join the two matriarchs.

Donovan's father pulled him aside, the two moving to a corner of the small home. The patriarch stared down at the painting Donovan had been working on, studying it intently.

"It's good," he said, impressed by his son's talents. "It's very good!"

"Thank you, Senior."

His father slapped him gently on the back. "You look happy, son."

"I am happy, Senior. I'm very happy."

"That's good. Your mother has been worried to death about you being here all alone with no family close by."

Donovan shook his head. "I don't know why."

Senior shrugged. "Donovan, you were always the quiet, studious one. You were always home while the others were all out running the streets doing what they do."

Donovan smiled. "Kendrick said Mom and the girls thought I was soft."

"Maybe not soft, but the most vulnerable. And that's only because they coddled you more than the other boys. You were always around and you let them. But I think these last few months, your mother's been able to see that your quiet strength has been a formidable resource. And I just wanted to tell you how proud I am of you, son!"

Donovan smiled as his father hugged him. "Thank you, Senior!"

"So when are you going to tell your mother that you don't plan to come back home?"

Donovan shot his father a look, and the two men locked gazes. "How…?"

"Kendrick told me."

Donovan sighed softly. "How do you think Mom's going to take it?"

Senior shrugged. "You know your mother. She wants you all home, or close to home. She hates it when you and your brothers and sisters aren't close enough for her to love on you."

Donovan nodded. "I'll tell her," he said softly.

His father nodded. "I'll help soften the blow afterward," he said. "She'll be okay as long as she knows she can come visit anytime she wants."

Donovan smiled. "Mom knows she can always come see me!"

Gianna moved to Donovan's side. "I don't mean to interrupt…"

"Not at all, pretty lady! You're not interrupting us at all!" Senior hugged her, too.

Donovan pressed a kiss to her forehead. "What's up?"

"I just spoke to my father, and he and Carina want

to prepare dinner for everyone if you all don't have other plans."

"We'd love to meet your family," Katherine said, joining the conversation.

Tarah suddenly rushed in from outside. "I love Italy!" she exclaimed, jumping up and down excitedly. "Can I stay?"

Franco greeted them at the door, his own excitement shimmering in his bright blue eyes. Donovan introduced them all one by one.

"Franco, this is my oldest brother, Mason, and Mason's wife, Phaedra. My sister Maitlyn and her husband, Zakaria. My sister Katrina and her husband, Matthew Stallion. My brother Darryl and his wife, Camryn. My brother Kendrick and his wife, Vanessa. My brother Guy and his wife, Dahlia, and my sisters Kamaya and Tarah."

Franco hugged and kissed and shook hands with them all. *"Ciao! Ciao!"* he said as he pointed everyone to Carina and Graham. "This is Gianna's twin sister and her husband."

Lastly, Donovan introduced his parents. "And this is my mother, Katherine, and my father, Senior Boudreaux. Mom, Senior, this is Franco Martelli, Gianna's father."

Franco and Senior shook hands before Franco threw his arms around the man. "What a spectacular family!" he said.

He moved to stand in front of Katherine. *"Ciao, bella!* I see where your daughters get their beauty from."

He grabbed her hand and kissed the back of it, his lips lingering. "It is a pleasure to meet you," he said, batting his baby blue eyes at her.

"Down, Giusseppi. That's my queen you're kissing," Senior said, a teasing smirk on his face.

Everyone in the room laughed.

Katherine giggled. "Pay him no mind!" she said as she looped her arm through Senior's. "He's not jealous."

Franco laughed heartily. "With such a beautiful woman by his side, I would understand him being jealous!"

Katherine giggled, a deep blush darkening her cheeks. "Gianna, your father is quite the charmer! You two should fix him up with my new friend, Felice."

Gianna and Carina both laughed. Carina moved to give Donovan's mother a welcoming hug. "We've been trying to get him and Signora Rossi together for years!"

The two fathers shook hands, cementing their new friendship.

"This is a mighty fine place you have here," Senior said.

Franco grinned. "Thank you. We are very proud of it. You must let us show you around."

"Please," Gianna said. "I'd love to give you the tour."

"There's wine involved, right?" Tarah asked.

Franco nodded. "Much, much vino!"

"I'm in!" Tarah exclaimed, clapping her hands together excitedly.

Kamaya shook her head, holding up a palm. "Don't worry, Mom. I'll keep an eye on her." She gave Tarah a slight push, and the two sisters burst into laughter.

* * *

Hours later the Boudreaux and Martelli families were still laughing and sharing, telling tall tales about Donovan and Gianna. The couple leaned against each other, overwhelmed by the love and support, and mutually embarrassed by the attention.

"I like her!" Katherine said, her husband's arms wrapped warmly around her shoulders. "I really like her a lot!"

Senior nodded. "She's a sweet, sweet girl. Donovan's done good!"

"And she loves him! Just look at her face."

"Look at his! That boy is caught up something fierce."

There was a lull in the conversation as they sat watching their children. They were all basking in the moment, their time together much needed. Both knew that it would only be days before each of their offspring would be headed off in their own directions, back to the daily responsibilities that kept them apart. Pride shone across both their faces.

"May I join you?" Franco asked, moving to Senior's side.

"Of course," Katherine said with a bright smile.

Senior gestured for him to take a seat. "Still flirting with my woman, I see."

Franco chuckled. "I can't help myself," he said as he gave Katherine a wink.

Senior kissed his wife's cheek. "I'm a lucky man, Franco. A very lucky man!"

Across the way, Donovan was watching his parents. He smiled with amusement as he eyed them teasing each other. "Senior's being quite the romantic," he noted, gesturing with his head toward the two as his father kissed his mother.

"It's Tuscany!" Gianna said with a bright smile. "Everything is romantic here!"

Donovan nodded. He shifted forward in his seat, grabbing both her hands between his own. "Are you ready to marry me, Gianna Martelli?"

She met the intense look he was giving her. "Are you proposing, Donovan Boudreaux?"

Donovan suddenly slid down onto one knee, still holding tight to her fingers. He reached into the pocket of his jeans, and as if out of nowhere he held up a diamond ring in fourteen-karat white gold. The vintage setting was stunning, pavé-set diamonds along the top half of the stunning band and around a single three-carat round-cut stone.

Gianna gasped in surprise, her eyes wide with wonder. "Donovan!"

The room suddenly fell quiet, everyone turning to stare. Smiles were wide and abundant as the two families moved in closer, not wanting to miss a moment of the proposal.

"Gianna, I love you. I can't imagine my life without you. You move me in ways no other woman will ever move me. I want to devote my life to you. To us. To the family I hope we have. Will you marry me? Will you be my wife and the mother of my children?"

Tears spilled past Gianna's lashes as she nodded her head. "Yes!" she exclaimed as Donovan slipped the ring onto her left hand.

The room erupted into cheers as their families celebrated the moment, congratulations ringing in the air. The women all pressed in to admire the new piece of jewelry that adorned Gianna's hand.

Kamaya turned toward her mother. "Is that Grandma's ring?" she asked, her smile widening.

Katherine nodded, tossing her husband a look. "It is."

Senior met his daughter's stare. "Your brother was the only one who asked me for my mother's ring."

Katherine nodded. "Maitlyn had it cleaned and a larger diamond put in the setting for him."

Senior and Franco shook hands. "Congratulations, sir!"

"And to you, sir!"

Both men hugged Katherine.

Donovan's brothers shook his hand and slapped him on his back, each offering congratulations and advice. He hugged Gianna to his side, both overwhelmed by all the excitement. Gianna suddenly leaned in to whisper in his ear.

"Are you sure?" he asked, beaming with joy.

She nodded, kissing his lips.

Donovan waved his hand for everyone's attention. "I just want to say thank you to everyone," he said, his gaze sweeping over each of them. "Thank you all for being here. For supporting me. For all the love you've shown to me and Gianna," he said, pausing for a quick moment before speaking again. "Now, we're going to challenge you."

Gianna grinned, biting down on her bottom lip. "Carina, Maitlyn, all you girls. Since everyone is here, do you think you all can help us pull off a wedding by this Sunday?"

Maitlyn and Carina both jumped with excitement. Kamaya threw her arms around Tarah, who squealed with joy. Phaedra, Camryn, Dahlia and Vanessa all chimed in with glee. Everyone was chattering with enthusiasm.

Katherine laughed. "Baby girl, you don't have to worry about a thing! You're going to get the wedding of your dreams!"

Chapter 15

Donovan woke to Gianna standing in the center of the bed jumping up and down with excitement. Her early-morning exuberance brought a smile to his face as he rubbed the sleep from his eyes with both hands.

"Good morning, sleepyhead!"

He shifted his body upward in the bed, resting his back against the headboard. "Good morning," he said with a yawn. "Why are you up? It's too early to be so happy!"

She laughed as she continued to bounce up and down. "It's not early. It's almost eight o'clock. And I'm always happy. I'm in love, didn't you hear?"

He reached for her hand and pulled her down against him. He embraced her in a deep bear hug. "I hope he's a really great guy because you, beautiful lady, deserve a really great guy."

Gianna grinned. "My guy is the greatest guy in the whole wide world," she said as she kissed his cheek.

Donovan laughed. "So, what's on your agenda today?"

"I'm going to go find my wedding dress today."

His brow suddenly furrowed in confusion. "Why did I think that's what you disappeared to do yesterday?"

Gianna shrugged, Donovan missing the look that crossed her face. "No. I had some errands to run but not for my dress."

He still looked confused. "I could have sworn that's what Carina told me you two were headed out to do."

She smiled, that nervous twitch making her eye jump as she tried to brush it off. "Maybe that's what she thought your sister had planned for us, but we had other things to do first. So we're going today and I'm nervous."

"Why?"

"I'm scared that I won't be able to find the perfect dress off the rack that will be ready by Sunday."

"Don't be scared. You'll find the perfect dress, and you'll be even more beautiful in it."

She kissed him again. "What are you going to do today?"

Donovan hesitated for a moment. "I think I'm going to go to the university this morning. I just want to show my face and get some things ready for when I go back to teaching next week."

"Do you think you should go alone?"

"I think I'll be fine. If any of my family members want to come, I'll enjoy showing them the school." He changed the subject. "How are all the wedding plans going?"

"Your sisters are amazing! I can't believe what they've done so far. Maitlyn has thought of everything!"

"Maitlyn has contacts all around the world. If you want something done, she is definitely your go-to girl."

"She and Carina have become good friends, and she's been giving her some advice about renting the winery more for private functions and increasing that revenue stream. Carina's determined to make us the wedding destination of destination weddings!"

Donovan laughed. "That sounds like my sister."

"Well, all of our paperwork is done, and my father spoke to the priest and he's on board, so we are good to go as long as I find a dress."

He kissed that sweet spot beneath her chin. "Then you need to find a dress!"

Gianna shifted against him, straddling his body. Donovan closed his eyes as she began to rock her pelvis back and forth, savoring the sensation of his member rising between her legs. She ground herself against him, over and over again. Her touch was heated and inviting, and he felt himself lengthen and swell beneath her caresses.

Reaching out both hands, he slipped them beneath the top she wore, grabbing her breasts. The soft tissue filled his hands nicely as he gently teased her nipples until they were hard like rock candy and protruded against the fabric of her shirt. Her skin was heated and perspiration suddenly dampened his palms. Gianna continued to taunt his member, the lengthy protrusion like a steel rod between them.

"Do you like this?" she whispered as she reached a hand between his legs to stroke him.

"Don't tease me, Gianna," he said as he pulled at her nightclothes. He was suddenly anxious to settle himself deep inside her. "I've got to have me some!"

She giggled softly as she reached for a condom out of the nightstand drawer. "I'm very serious about wanting some, too, so you better hurry. Your sisters will be here in an hour!"

After Gianna and the girls were gone, Donovan headed toward the school. At the last minute he'd decided against asking any of his family to join him, wanting some time to himself to think. Feeling like the stars had aligned perfectly, he sang to himself, the lyrics to a love song ringing through the air.

Gianna was going to be his wife. The reality of that made his heart skip. As he thought of the vows they would soon take, he hoped he could capture with words the wealth of emotion that had been flooding his spirit on a daily basis.

He wanted to be the best husband he could be. He'd promised Franco that his daughter would want for nothing, and Donovan had meant every word. Protecting and caring for Gianna had become a mission, and it would be a lifelong journey he couldn't wait to explore. She was his, and he felt immensely blessed.

He was so absorbed in thoughts of her and him together that he wasn't paying any attention to the other cars parked in the employee spaces at the school. Inside, he waved hello, stopping to have a quick conversation with Dr. Northway before heading to his office. Everyone was excited to welcome him back and disappointed that he wasn't going to officially be back for another few days.

His desk was stacked with papers that needed his attention, and as he flipped casually through them he couldn't begin to fathom how he was going to get them graded before his wedding. As he organized what he needed to do and how he needed to do it, there was a knock on his door.

He looked up just as the door opened. "Yes?"

One of the young men from his linear equations class poked his head in. "Dr. Boudreaux, *buongiorno!*"

"*Buongiorno*, Marco! How are you?"

"*Bene grazie*, signor. I wanted to welcome you back."

Donovan smiled. "I appreciate that, Marco."

"I will see you in class today, no?"

"Not today," Donovan said with a shake of his head. "I will be here on Monday."

The boy nodded. "Very good, signor! I will see you then."

For the next hour Donovan entertained students and instructors alike, all stopping to express their happiness with his return and their regrets for everything he'd been put through. Realizing that he was going to get little accomplished, he packed up the stacks of paperwork and dropped them into his attaché case, then headed to his car.

Sophie was leaning against his car, her arms crossed over her chest. Her car was parked beside his, the backseat loaded with boxes and books from her office. She stood upright as he approached, and it wasn't until he was standing before her that he noticed her black eye and swollen face. His eyes widened.

"Sophie, what happened to you?"

She shook her head, and when she went to speak he realized her jaw was wired shut, her teeth clenched tightly together. "I just…wanted…to apologize…to you…for my part…in what happened." The words came slowly, barely audible.

Donovan nodded. "I appreciate that."

She rolled her eyes as she took a breath. "I hear… you are…getting…married."

"I am," he said, suddenly curious that word of their wedding had traveled so quickly.

"Good…luck…with that!" she said as she tossed up a hand. She turned to get into her vehicle.

Donovan called after her.

"Yes?"

"May I ask how you broke your jaw?"

The woman paused as she thought back to her last encounter with Alessandra, her prized student turning on her. She'd dodged the first punch the young girl had thrown, but the second had caught her in just the right spot. Sophie's eyes were angry slits as she met his stare. "Yes," she said. "I…ran into…the wrong…woman."

Donovan narrowed his gaze on Gianna's face. Carina sat beside him. Both women looked as if they'd been caught red-handed. His tone was scolding as he shared the details of his encounter with Sophie Mugabe.

"That's a shame!" Carina said, her voice quivering ever so slightly.

Across the room Franco shook his head, he and Graham grinning broadly.

Donovan had to ask. "Did you break that woman's jaw, Gianna?"

Gianna tossed up her hands. "Why do you think that I had something to do with what happened to her?"

Donovan tilted his head slightly. "Did you break her jaw, Carina?"

"It wasn't me!"

"So where did you two disappear to the other day when I thought you were dress shopping?" He glanced from Gianna to Carina and back.

The two sisters exchanged a look. Neither said a word.

Donovan shook his head at Gianna. "That right hook of yours again, huh?"

Gianna scoffed. "Why are you assuming I busted that woman in her face? Not that she didn't deserve it for what she put you through, but still…"

Tarah laughed. "I'm so glad it's not me this time. I used to always get blamed for everything!"

Guy laughed. "That's because usually it's always you doing something you shouldn't be doing!"

Tarah rolled her eyes. "Well, I'm not unhappy that woman got her jaw broke. She spread lies about Donovan, and if I'd seen her I might have popped her, too!"

Katherine laughed. "So would I!" she exclaimed.

The men all shook their heads. Donovan pulled Gianna into a hug, and she allowed herself to melt into the embrace. She tilted her head to stare up at him.

"Are you mad?" she asked.

He smiled and shook his head. "Just don't do it again," he said.

She sighed in frustration. "I'm telling you, I didn't do a thing!"

Carina laughed. "Did I forget to tell you that her nickname used to be Little Mike, for Mike Tyson!"

Franco tapped his chest as he tossed Donovan a wink. "She got that from me!"

The twins were enjoying a moment of quiet where it was just the two of them, alone together. Carina had pinned her sister's hair in an updo, and was delighting in how very beautiful she looked. They glanced at each other and smiled.

"Are you still mad at me?" Carina said softly, moving to sit by Gianna's side.

Gianna laughed. "How could I ever be mad at you, Sissy?"

"I just don't want Donovan thinking you attacked that woman. We both know there's no way you could have done something like that. I mean, you do have a perfect alibi. You were with me."

"He doesn't. And even if he did, once he finds out the truth, it will all be good."

Carina smiled. She pressed a hand over her abdomen, tears filling her eyes. "I'm having a baby, Sissy! Can you believe it? Me? With a baby!"

Gianna laughed as she gave her sister a warm hug. "You're going to be a wonderful mother! And I'm blessed to have been there at the doctor with you when you found out." She squeezed Carina's hands. "Now, when are you going to tell Graham?"

"After the wedding. I didn't want my joy to overshadow your joy. This is your moment, and I want it to be the very best day of your whole life."

Gianna shook her head. "Tell your husband, Sissy. We have so much to celebrate, and with all this love around us there's no reason for both of us not to share our joys with everybody."

The two women embraced again, pulling back to wipe each other's tears.

"Don't cry," Carina admonished. "You're going to ruin your makeup."

"Donovan doesn't care if I wear makeup!"

"So do I get a pass now for the way I fixed you and Donovan up? Am I totally forgiven?"

Gianna nodded. "Completely. If it wasn't for you, I wouldn't be this happy!"

There was a sudden knock on the door. Both women turned to stare just as Maitlyn peeked her head inside the room. "I don't mean to interrupt, but it's time to go get you married. Are you ready to get into your gown?"

The two sisters connected gazes one last time. Gianna took a deep breath and held it for a quick minute as Carina squeezed her hand.

Carina waved all of the Boudreaux women into the room. "She's ready!"

Donovan was nervous as he stood at the front of the little country chapel, his brothers by his side. They were all dressed in designer, blue silk suits, white dress shirts and printed navy blue ties with thin orange and white stripes.

Flowers in every shade of the rainbow decorated the small space, their sweet scent billowing through the warm air. A trio of violins played sweetly, the soft lilt of music dancing with the breeze that blew through the open windows and doors.

Father Cesare Balducci, the Martelli family's priest, stood on Donovan's other side. He was a tall and slender man who looked regal in his robes as he held a leather-bound Bible in his hands.

Father Balducci tapped Donovan's arm. "We are ready to begin," he said softly as he tilted his head toward the back of the church.

The violin tune suddenly shifted, the prelude to the "Bridal Chorus" announcing Gianna's arrival. Family and friends and people from the village all turned at the same time to watch the procession down the aisle.

Tarah led the way, Kamaya, Katrina, Maitlyn and Carina following. They wore strapless, tea-length gowns that bore a soft floral print. Each was stunning, with French braids complementing their faces. Even Carina's short locks had been braided with extensions.

Donovan was grinning from ear to ear, clenching his fists together tightly. He took a deep breath and then a second as Carina and his sisters all greeted him with a smile.

Then, there she was! Gianna was a vision to behold, an apparition of magnanimous proportions. Donovan was in awe of just how exquisite she was. Her gown was everything she had wanted it to be. It was a strapless, slim A-line silhouette with a corset closure. It had a sophisticated overlay of vintage lace and featured an asymmetrical satin panel that was gathered and wrapped across her waistline to create a figure-flattering effect. A simple satin bow rested gently at the side of her front hip, accentuating her wisp of a waist. As she walked down the aisle in his direction, Donovan cried, tears falling easily over his cheeks.

The ceremony attested to their faith and love for each other. With their family serving as witnesses, they vowed to love and honor each other. Gianna's tears came when Donovan recited the vows he'd written.

"Gianna, since the first day I laid eyes on you, you have made me feel more complete, more alive, and you have shown me the true meaning of happiness. I am a better man with you by my side than I can ever be without you. So today, in front of you, and those we love most, I take you to be my partner, loving what I know of you, and trusting what I do not yet know, excited to discover the woman you will become.

"I promise to respect you as my equal, and to recognize that your interests, desires and needs are as important as my own. I promise to laugh with you when times are good. To endure with you when they are bad. I will grow old with you, happily! I promise to fall more in love with you each and every day. Today, tomorrow, and every day I give you my hand, my heart and my love without condition, completely and forever."

Gianna giggled like a girl as he slipped her wedding band on her finger. She swiped the tears from her cheek and cleared her voice as the priest gestured for her to speak. Gianna had balked at writing her own vows and had only agreed after much prodding. Her vows, short, sweet and uniquely Gianna, brought joy and laughter to Donovan's heart.

"Donovan Boudreaux, I…choose…you!" She winked at him as she placed a gold band on his ring finger, then leaned down to kiss the back of his hand.

With the exchange of rings, Father Balducci pronounced them husband and wife, and the room erupted in cheers. Without giving it a thought, Donovan swept her off her feet, lifting her into his arms. He kissed her mouth as Gianna wrapped her arms around his neck. Then he carried her back down the aisle and out the church doors, their family following behind them.

The reception was held in the Martelli fields, a carpet of lush green grass surrounded by fields of red poppies. Rustic wooden tables draped with red runners sat beneath large arches of green ivy. Floral-covered spheres in bright orange, yellow and red hung from the arches, and the tables were decorated with gold-trimmed plates with the finest crystal and gold tableware. A dance floor had been set up on the lawn, and a small band was playing all of their favorite songs. The bright blue sky and the most incredible weather proved to be the perfect backdrop for their celebration.

Gathered together, the family posed for a multitude of photographs to capture the memories. Mason's wife, Phaedra, was their personal wedding photographer. Their guests dined on platters of roasted chicken, potatoes and vegetables, the meal completed with Gianna's favorite lemon-filled cake and bottles of her father's wine. Donovan and Gianna couldn't stop grinning, everything about their day sheer perfection.

Hours later Gianna pulled at Donovan's arm. "Come dance with me again," she pleaded.

Donovan laughed. "I need a break, sweetheart! I can't keep up with you."

Gianna feigned a pout. "I'll have to find another man to dance with me, then."

He nodded, pointing toward his brothers. "Take your pick!"

She leaned in to kiss his lips. As she did, she slipped a folded note into his pocket.

Slipping his hand into the jacket, he gave her a curious look. "What's this?"

"Read your mail," she said as she winked at him. She danced away, her hips twisting in a teasing shimmy.

Pulling the note out of his pocket, he stepped away from the crowd and began to read.

My dearest Donovan,
Just hours ago I became Mrs. Gianna Boudreaux, and now I wear your family name proudly. I am blessed to have your love, and I am honored to stand by your side as your partner and companion.

I pledge myself to you, heart and soul. I promise to be with you in happiness and strife. To love you in richness and debt. To be faithful, even when we are old and dull.

Thank you for trusting me with your heart. I

do not take that responsibility lightly. I will cherish you until we each take our last breath and then on into eternity.

You, my darling, have given me my happily-ever-after, and for the very first time I can honestly say I know love because of you.

Always and forever,

Gianna

PS: I think it would be good business for us to write a book of love letters. We'll call it *Tuscan Heat*. I've written the first. I'll wait for you to write the next.

Immeasurable joy painted Donovan's expression. Across the yard, Gianna met his stare and smiled. She lifted her hand and blew him a kiss. Pretending to catch it in his palm, he drew his closed fist to his heart and whispered the words *I love you!*

* * * * *

REQUEST YOUR FREE BOOKS!

2 FREE NOVELS PLUS 2 FREE GIFTS!

KIMANI™ ROMANCE

Love's ultimate destination!

KROM15

THE WORLD IS BETTER WITH

Romance

Harlequin has everything from contemporary, passionate and heartwarming to suspenseful and inspirational stories.

Whatever your mood, we have a romance just for you!

Connect with us to find your next great read, special offers and more.

f /HarlequinBooks

🐦 @HarlequinBooks

www.HarlequinBlog.com

www.Harlequin.com/Newsletters

HARLEQUIN®

A Romance FOR EVERY MOOD™

www.Harlequin.com

SERIESHALOAD2015

April Knight crouched next to a young girl who sat with a cello positioned between her spaced knees. The large, slightly scarred instrument dwarfed her, but the teen didn't seem intimidated. She looked on intently as, with her signature calmness, April corrected whatever misstep the girl had just made on the piece they were practicing. She instructed her on how to glide the bow along the taut strings. The result was fluid. A mesmerizing note resonated throughout the space.

Once she was done assisting the room's lone cello player, April returned to the front of the room. When she turned and spotted him, her face lit up with a smile. Several of the students—those who were not engrossed in reading their sheet music—turned to see who had captured their teacher's attention. April held up a hand and mouthed *five minutes*.

Damien nodded. Leaning a shoulder along the door-jamb, he folded his arms across his chest, crossed his ankles and studied the woman standing at the helm of the class. It had been months since he'd seen her, from the time when he had run into her at a Christmas party that one of his clients had invited him to at a loft in the Warehouse District. That had been what? Six months ago?

He'd arrived late, and April had been on her way out. Their encounter had been nothing more than a quick hug and profuse thanks from April for the donation Damien had given to A Fresh Start. They'd both promised each other that they would meet for coffee so they could catch up, but whenever he'd thought about calling her over the past six months something else had always come up.

Five minutes came and went, but Damien didn't dare interrupt April as she coached her pupils through a delicate piece. Besides, watching her in action was too entertaining to bring it to an end.

And to Damien's surprise he was watching her with more interest than he ever remembered watching his friend before. She wore soft yellow capri pants that hit just past her calves, a smart choice on this warm day. She probably had the heat and humidity in mind when she chose to pair it with the sleeveless white button-down blouse, but Damien thought it was the right choice for an entirely different reason.

Don't miss
PASSION'S SONG by Farrah Rochon,
available February 2016 wherever
Harlequin® Kimani Romance™ books and ebooks are sold.